BASED ON THE GROUNDBREAKING
MYSTERY SERIES BY **EVE ZAREMBA**

WORK FOR A MILLION

THE GRAPHIC NOVEL

AMANDA DEIBERT

ILLUSTRATED BY
SELENA GOULDING

McCLELLAND & STEWART

Introduction

by EVE ZAREMBA

Work for a Million, my second novel about Helen Keremos, lesbian Private Investigator, came out in 1987. It was written when what is now the past was still in the future. I wrote it in the backroom of my used bookstore in Toronto. I was 56 years old then, 90 in 2020.

Up until a couple of years ago, I had no clue that one of my Keremos books would be translated into a graphic novel. I knew little about the genre of adult comics and graphic novels. And what I did know wasn't altogether positive. Since then, I have been thoroughly re-educated.

This graphic adaptation by Amanda and Selena of *Work for a Million* follows closely the plot, characters, and dialogue of the novel, necessarily simplified and shortened. The result of their creative effort is fully in the spirit of the original. And I love seeing Helen Keremos on the page, not just in words.

My main interest as a writer is in Helen Keremos, the first lesbian private investigator in detective fiction. Helen Keremos embodies the eighties dyke persona. She is primarily an independent woman, an outsider, skeptical of all popular mythology and suspicious of all stereotypes. Keremos doesn't act "nice" as a woman should and isn't bound by conventional standards of behaviour or morality. Her dynamic presence commands attention, also sometimes negative reaction. She is attractive to women and not just potential lovers, and gets along well with men she respects. Keremos has little interest in sectarian and identity politics, but her instinctive commitment to women runs deep. Helen's main allegiance is to her community and friends, to whom she is fiercely loyal, and to her work as a professional investigator.

Note: by definition, a private investigator is politically incorrect.

Foreword

by **AMANDA DEIBERT**

As a little girl who grew up devouring mysteries and wishing she could be James Bond, Eve Zaremba's novel *Work for a Million* hit me in a sweet spot. Here is the action-packed, street-smart life of Helen Keremos, a private investigator who goes toe-to-toe with any man and can also understand the unspoken undercurrents of the lives of the women around her. I especially love that she's a butch woman in her 40s. After devouring the book, I couldn't wait to dive in and help bring this smart, savvy detective into the world of graphic novels. My first priority in writing was to do justice to Eve's incredible story. It was important to me that any changes I made to plot or characters kept the essence of the original work, and collaborating with Selena Goulding was a dream. Selena's gorgeous art really brought things to life. You can feel the sexual tension in Helen and Sonia's body language.

Another thing that was so important to me was keeping the essence of Toronto during this certain time period. For this, Selena and I relied on research and also information from Eve and her amazing wife Ottie Lockey, who filled us in on any details from a time before Selena's and mine. I remember a particular "Amanda, have you ever… driven a stick shift?" email that led to me confessing my college girlfriend taught me on a road trip and I hadn't really done it since.

Luckily, Selena is also in Toronto, so I knew I could lean on her for visual accuracy. I'm not from Toronto, but my love of the city makes this story all the more special to me. I made my first visit to Toronto when I was a university student. I was travelling with conservative family members and I was still in the closet. My first day in Toronto just happened to be the day same-sex marriage was legalized in Ontario. Everywhere I went, newspaper covers with happy couples smiled back at me. It was the first time I truly felt like maybe the future could possibly be brighter for me. It wasn't my country, and I couldn't say a word to anyone, but those smiling faces of couples in Toronto made me feel less alone. I grabbed a newspaper and hid it in my suitcase as a reminder of what *could* be.

And now here I am, a legally married lesbian mother with a family and the privilege of adapting a work by an out lesbian writer with an unapologetically dyke lead set right there in the heart of Toronto. I feel so fortunate to be a part of this—to work with Selena in bringing this graphic novel to life, and to be trusted to adapt Eve's work. I get to write in a more representative world. I get to write stories that reflect my life and my experiences because of the trailblazers who came before me. People like Eve and characters like Helen. I'm proud of the work Selena and I have done. I'm grateful to all those involved who worked so hard to bring it to life. I hope you fall in love with Helen as deeply as I did.

Dramatis Personae

HELEN KEREMOS: a world-class detective in her early 40s, tall with short dark hair and a face that oozes confidence—a woman you'd describe as "handsome." Helen's sharp eyes miss nothing, including any beautiful woman in the room, but her job as a detective always comes first and… she's damn good at it.

SONIA DEERFIELD: a talented young singer with supermodel good looks and fiery red hair, Sonia has career ambitions in spades and a huge heart. She takes care of everyone in her life—but are they taking advantage of her generous nature? As she's only in her mid-20s, she may seem a bit naïve, but mess with anyone in her inner circle and you'll find she's anything but weak. She seems intensely drawn to Helen, the only person in her life who doesn't "need" her.

ARTHUR SEDGWICK: The senior partner in the law firm, Sedgwick, Sedgwick, McClelland, Potter and Bono. Sonia's attorney. Arthur is a small, spare man in his late 50s with icy blue eyes and perfectly understated-yet-impeccable clothing. This is a man who oozes power. To be in a room with Arthur Sedgwick is to know you are truly insignificant. His manner is always gracious, but as with any truly powerful man, there's an undercurrent of danger.

BETTY GRELICK: A blonde in her 30s, Betty dresses with care to mask her insecurities. She adores her best friend Sonia—seems unaware that said adoration is a latent crush. She's possessively jealous. She's also Sonia's agent.

LEW DAVIES: A short, dark man in his 40s with rumpled clothing, Lew is Sonia's arranger, vocal coach, and also general assistant. He lives to take care of her and meet all her needs, but the truth is he needs Sonia a lot more than she needs him.

ALEX EDWARDS: An attractive woman in her early 40s, Alex is Helen's right-hand woman and, at one time, almost her lover. But they found they work together far too well to ruin that with an affair. She has connections all over Toronto and knows how to use them to get dirt on anyone at anytime.

WALT LAUKER: Sonia's ex-husband. Walt is a good-looking man of 30 with shaggy brown hair, pale skin, and sky-blue eyes. He also has a flair for the dramatic and the laid-back, casual style of a playboy without the money. His devil-may-care attitude, artsy, eccentric persona and winning smile hide his true feelings at any moment.

KARL DEERFIELD: Sonia's uncle. Karl is a trim, middle-aged man in his 50s with a vaguely military bearing. He comes across as a doting, if flighty, uncle on the surface.

BEN BONO: Another lawyer who works under Arthur Sedgwick. Ben is desperately in love with Sonia, but also desperately under Arthur's grip.

DETECTIVE SERGEANT FRANCIS MALORY: A balding man in his late 30s, Malory projects a bored self-assurance that actually pays off in brightness. He gets in Helen's way more often than not.

NATE OTTOLINE: If Alex is Helen's Gal Friday, Nate is her Guy Saturday. He's a good-looking, confident, gay Black man who knows anyone and everyone in town and exactly what it is they don't want anyone else to know. He's a loyal friend and isn't afraid to get his hands dirty when needed.

TOMMY BURROWS: Middle-aged, a well-dressed man with a corporate feel. A lacky for Arthur Sedgwick.

CHESTER: In his late 30s, a hotel detective. Chester wears cheap, ill-fitting suits and has an even cheaper personality. He'll give you whatever you need… unless you aren't the highest bidder.

WORK
FOR A
MILLION

DOWNTOWN TORONTO.

WHEN CAN I SEE YOU AGAIN?

TONIGHT WAS A LOT OF FUN, ROSE, BUT I'M HEADING BACK TO VANCOUVER. I'VE GOT A NEW TRUCK AND THE OPEN ROAD IS CALLING MY NAME.

WANT COMPANY?

OH HONEY, IT'S NOT THAT KINDA TRIP. I'LL BE GONE AT LEAST SIX MONTHS. I'LL CALL YOU WHEN I'M BACK IN TOWN.

IMPERIAL PALACE HOTEL, JARVIS STREET.

HELLO, SONIA SPEAKING.

YOU KNOW WHAT THEY SAY, 'MONEY IS THE ROOT OF ALL EVIL.' IT'D BE A GOOD IDEA TO GET RID OF YOURS BEFORE SOMETHIN' BAD HAPPENS.

I'VE TOLD YOU BEFORE. YOU'RE NOT GETTING A CENT.

you can make this stop whenever you're ready.

OH MY GOD. HOW DID THEY GET INSIDE?

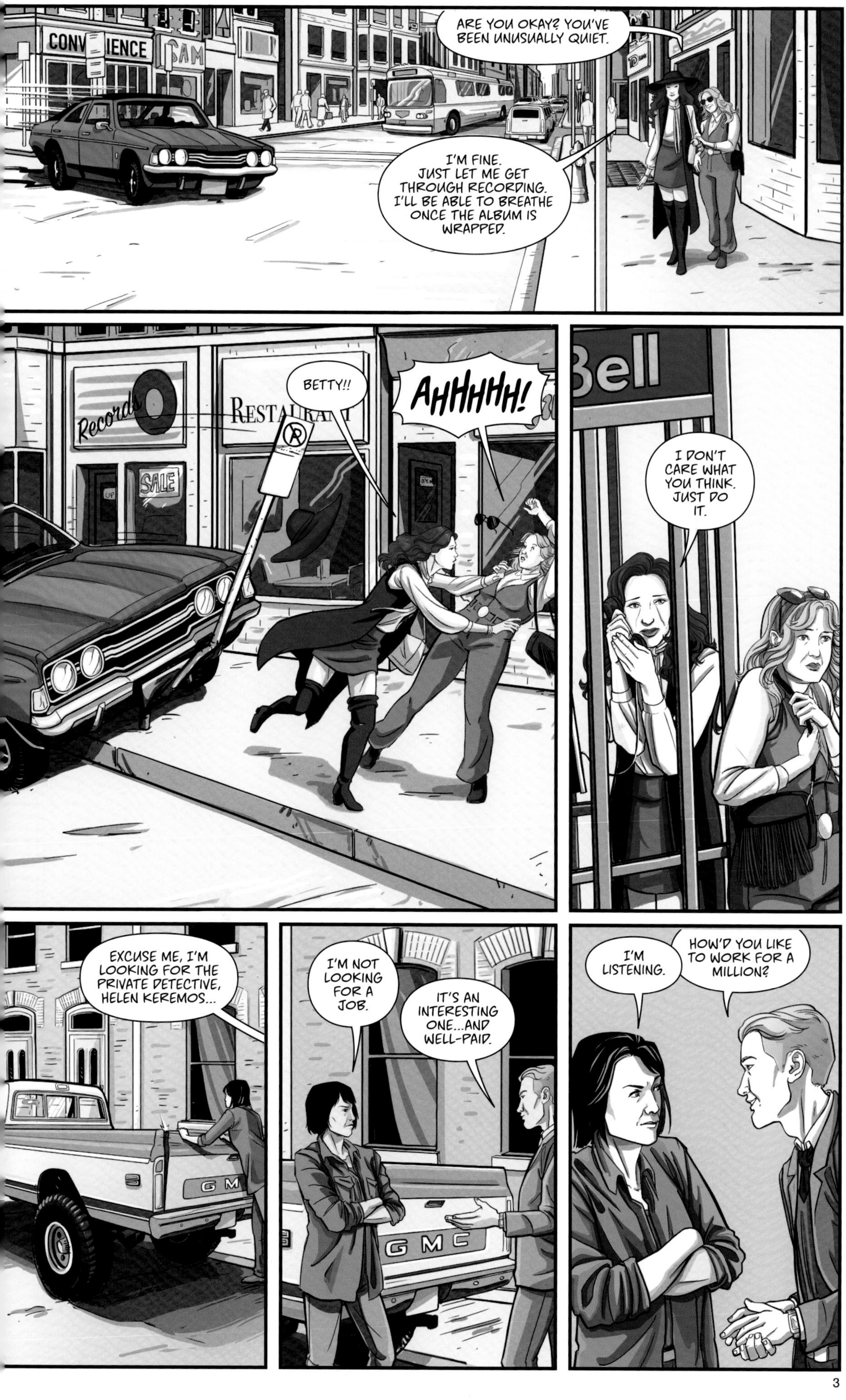
CONV IENCE
SAM
ARE YOU OKAY? YOU'VE BEEN UNUSUALLY QUIET.
I'M FINE. JUST LET ME GET THROUGH RECORDING. I'LL BE ABLE TO BREATHE ONCE THE ALBUM IS WRAPPED.
Records
SALE
BETTY!!
AHHHHH!
Bell
I DON'T CARE WHAT YOU THINK. JUST DO IT.
EXCUSE ME, I'M LOOKING FOR THE PRIVATE DETECTIVE, HELEN KEREMOS...
GMC
I'M NOT LOOKING FOR A JOB.
IT'S AN INTERESTING ONE...AND WELL-PAID.
GMC
I'M LISTENING.
HOW'D YOU LIKE TO WORK FOR A MILLION?

DING!

SEDGWICK, SEDGWICK, McCLELLAND, POTTER & BONO

ATTORNEYS AT LAW

SMBP

926 BAY S...
TORONTO ON M5S...6
555-926-1990...

TIME TO SEE WHICH ONE OF US IS THE SHMUCK.

THIS IS WHERE I GET OFF.

OH... MY.

MR. SEDGWICK IS EXPECTING YOU.

GWICK, SEDGWICK,
...ELLAND, POTTER & BONO
ATTORN... ...LAW

MS. KEREMOS, BEFORE WE BEGIN, I NEED YOUR ASSURANCE THIS CONVERSATION WILL BE KEPT CONFIDENTIAL... WHETHER YOU ACCEPT THIS ASSIGNMENT OR NOT.

I CAN'T PROMISE ANYTHING BLINDLY... EVEN SILENCE. BUT I CAN TELL YOU THERE'S A REASON I'VE STAYED IN BUSINESS SO LONG.

BEN, GO AHEAD.

HAVE YOU HEARD OF MISS SONIA DEERFIELD?

THAT LOTTERY WINNER I'VE BEEN READING ABOUT IN ALL THE PAPERS? SHE'S A PRETTY, ASPIRING SINGER, RIGHT?

THE PAPERS DON'T DO MISS DEERFIELD JUSTICE. SHE'S ON HER WAY TO STARDOM, EVERY ONE OF US HERE IS CERTAIN OF IT.

SO, SHE'S MY CLIENT?

SINCE THE LOTTERY, SONIA'S BEEN HARASSED, THREATENED, AND HAD ATTEMPTS ON HER LIFE.

HERE ARE THE PHONE LOGS. ALL TO SONIA'S UNLISTED NUMBER. THEY STARTED AS VAGUE THREATS—

DID YOU ADVISE HER THAT PHONE THREATS ARE A POLICE MATTER?

WE DID, BUT FRANKLY, SONIA DOESN'T TRUST THE POLICE. BUT MORE RECENTLY, HER HOME WAS BROKEN INTO AND SHE WAS ALMOST RUN DOWN BY A CAR—

AND *STILL* NO POLICE? AREN'T YOU TAKING A HELL OF A BIG RISK?

THAT'S WHY WE CALLED YOU. AND THEN LAST NIGHT—

"I KNEW I SHOULDN'T HAVE LEFT HER ALONE."

SURE YOU DON'T WANT ME TO STAY?

MR. BONO!

ON THE COUCH! FOR YOUR PROTECTION!

I'M FINE. I JUST WANT TO TAKE A SHOWER AND GET SOME SLEEP. I'LL CALL YOU IN THE MORNING TO LET YOU KNOW I SURVIVED.

THAT'S NOT FUNNY.

I CAN TAKE CARE OF MYSELF, I PROMISE.

CLICK

♪ YOU ARE THE ONLY ONE FOR ME...LA, DA, DA, DA, DEE... ♪

♪ ...YOU STOLE MY HEART... ♪

CLICK

BEN?

AHHHHHHHH!

HELP! HELP!

SHE DIDN'T GET A GOOD LOOK?

JUST SHADOWS. SHE WAS SO STARTLED SHE CAN'T EVEN TELL US HIS HEIGHT.

I'M EXPENSIVE.

THAT'S FINE AS LONG AS YOU'RE WORTH IT.

WE WANT YOU TO START RIGHT AWAY. YOU CAN MOVE INTO SONIA'S PLACE TODAY. SHE'S WITH HER VOCAL COACH, LEW DAVIES, UNTIL—

NOT SO FAST. BEFORE I SAY YES, I NEED TO MEET HER. ALONE.

I'VE CERTAINLY STAYED IN WORSE. NOT BY MUCH, THOUGH.

IMPERIAL PALACE

HOTEL

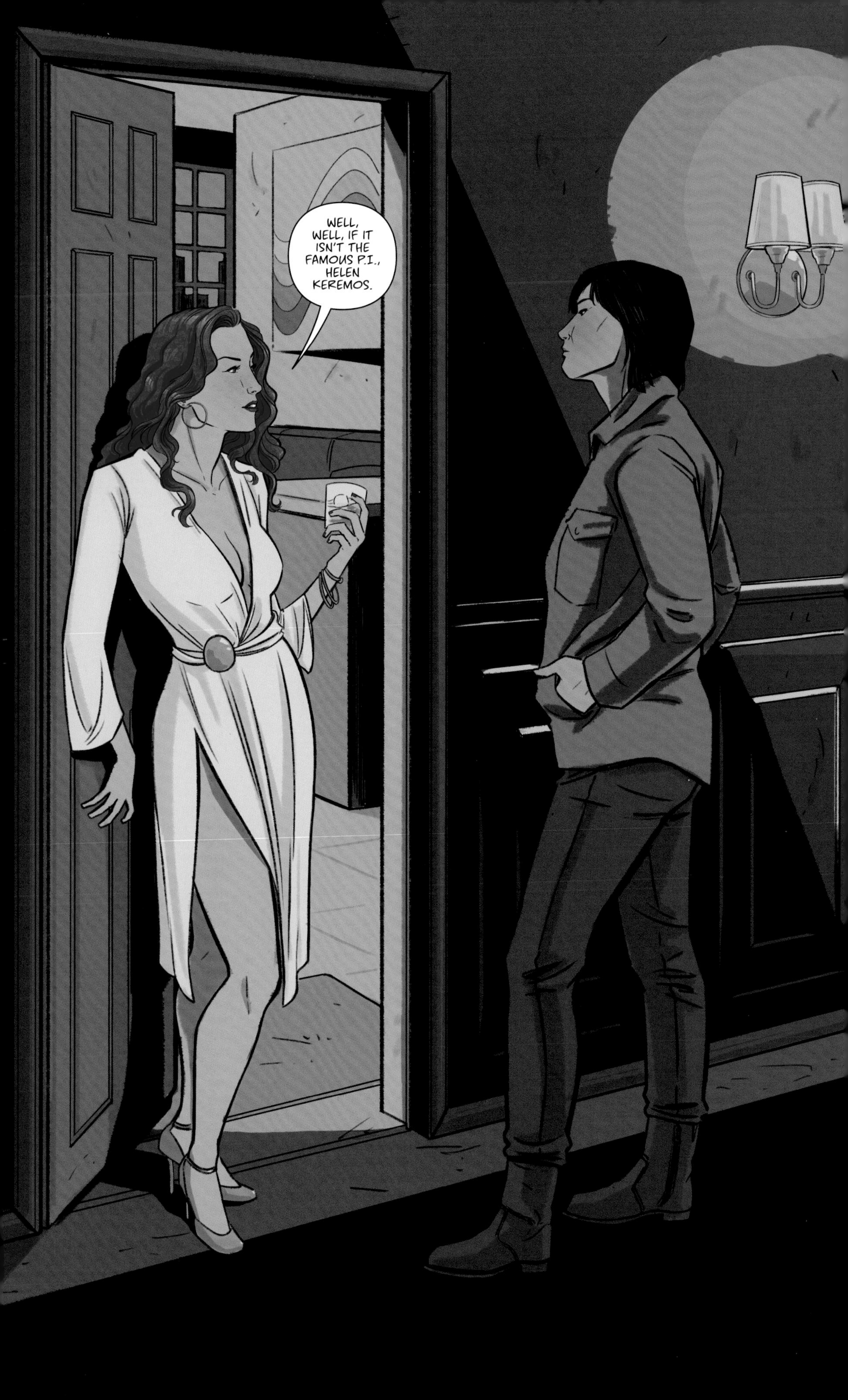
WELL, WELL, IF IT ISN'T THE FAMOUS P.I., HELEN KEREMOS.

I HEARD ABOUT YOU FROM MY DEAR FRIEND, SALLY RICHMOND IN VANCOUVER. SHE SAID YOU HELPED HER OUT OF A JAM... AND SHE DESCRIBED YOU PERFECTLY.

I HOPE THAT'S A GOOD THING.

YOU ARE JUST WHO I NEED. CAN I GET YOU A DRINK?

SCOTCH. ONE CUBE.

I DON'T NORMALLY DRINK THIS EARLY IN THE DAY, BUT... MY NERVES. OH, I'M SO GLAD YOU'RE HERE. NOW I'LL BE ABLE TO SLEEP AT NIGHT. CAN YOU MOVE IN RIGHT AWAY?

I HAVEN'T AGREED TO ANYTHING YET. WHAT DO YOU WANT FROM ME OTHER THAN JUST MY BEING HERE?

I NEED SOMEONE TO TRUST. I THOUGHT WINNING A MILLION DOLLARS WAS A DREAM COME TRUE. I FINALLY HAVE THE MONEY TO LET MY MUSIC CAREER BE WHAT I WANT IT TO BE...

AND THAT HASN'T BEEN TRUE?

THE MONEY ONLY SPEEDS THINGS UP, MAKES IT HARDER TO KNOW WHAT THE HELL IS GOING ON.

EVERY DAY I FEEL LESS COMFORTABLE WITH MY LIFE. I COULD'VE HANDLED THE CHANGES, BUT THEN THESE PHONE CALLS... I KNOW HOW THIS SOUNDS. I KNOW I SHOULD BE GRATEFUL, AND I AM...

YOU DON'T SOUND UNGRATEFUL. YOU SOUND LIKE A PERSON IN A TOUGH SPOT.

IT'S JUST TOO MUCH. I WANT OUT! BUT THEN THERE ARE ALL THESE PEOPLE WHO DEPEND ON ME...

WHO DEPENDS ON YOU?

OH, MY AGENT BETTY AND MY VOCAL COACH, LEW. THEY'RE BOTH DEAR FRIENDS. AND THEN, OF COURSE, THERE'S ARTHUR SEDGWICK, MY LAWYER. HE'S BEEN A STRONG ADVOCATE FOR MY CAREER, LINING UP RECORDING CONTRACTS.

THEY'RE ALL VERY SUPPORTIVE, BUT I FEEL SO ALONE.

NO FAMILY? LOVERS?

MY PARENTS ARE GONE. I HAVE AN ESTRANGED SISTER AND AN UNCLE WHO IS NOT IN MY LIFE. AND I WAS MARRIED FOR A WHILE.

WALT AND I SPLIT UP A COUPLE YEARS AGO, BUT WE'VE STAYED FRIENDLY. NO BAD BLOOD. AND NOW THERE'S BEN BONO.

HE MENTIONED YOU WERE SEEING EACH OTHER.

WELCOME TO Fabulous LAS VEGAS NEVADA

HE WANTS TO MARRY ME. IT'S COMPLICATED.

BECAUSE THE FEELINGS AREN'T MUTUAL?

IT'S ALL SO CONFUSING. I FEEL LIKE I'M UNRAVELLING AND I HATE IT.

I'M USUALLY A VERY TOGETHER PERSON. NOW I JUST FEEL AFRAID ALL THE TIME. THAT'S WHY IT WOULD BE SO NICE TO HAVE A STRONG WOMAN AROUND. I BET NOTHING SCARES YOU.

OH I GET SCARED, BUT NOT NEARLY AS SCARED AS WHOEVER IS DOING THIS TO YOU SHOULD FEEL RIGHT NOW...

DOES THIS MEAN YOU'RE TAKING THE JOB?

SURE. YOU'VE JUST HIRED ME. I'LL MOVE IN TONIGHT.

THANK YOU! I FEEL SAFER ALREADY.

GIVE ME A COUPLE HOURS, I'LL BE BACK WITH MY TOOTHBRUSH BY 7:30.

I WAS ALL PREPARED TO PINE AWAY WHILE YOU WERE IN VANCOUVER AND NOW SUDDENLY I'VE GOT A JOB?

PINING AWAY FOR ME, EH ALEX? AND WHAT WAS THE NAME OF THE ATTRACTIVE YOUNG LADY YOU BROUGHT WITH YOU TO MY GOING AWAY PARTY LAST WEEK?

HA HA! SINCE WHEN HAS EITHER OF US CARED ENOUGH TO REMEMBER NAMES?

AND *THAT* IS EXACTLY WHY WE MAKE BETTER BUSINESS ASSOCIATES THAN LOVERS. SPEAKING OF WHICH, LET'S GET INTO THE CASE.

POOR LITTLE RICH GIRL IS IN TROUBLE? SO WHAT? IT'S MOST LIKELY HER EX-HUSBAND. YOU WOULDN'T BE CANCELLING YOUR BIG TRIP IF THERE WEREN'T...OTHER INTERESTS IN THIS CASE.

YOUR CONFIDENCE IN MY PROFESSIONALISM IS TOUCHING.

SHE ASKED FOR YOU BY NAME. JUST BE SURE SHE'S NOT AFTER YOUR BEAUTIFUL BODY... OR YOU HERS.

YEAH, YEAH. FIRST I NEED YOUR CONNECTIONS TO CHECK SONIA'S SUITE FOR BUGS. SOMEONE IS GETTING INFO THAT ISN'T IN THE GOSSIP COLUMNS.

NO PROBLEM.

THEN RUN A CHECK ON ARTHUR SEDGWICK, BEN BONO, BETTY GRELICK, LEW DAVIES, AND THE EX, WALT LAUKER.

AND WHAT SHALL I DO IN MY SPARE TIME?

COMPLAIN. WHAT ELSE?

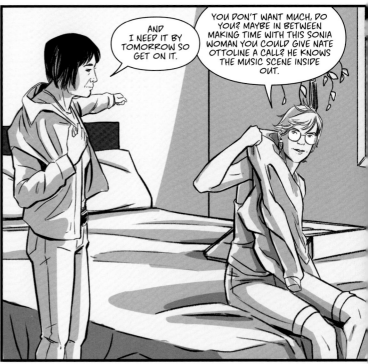

AND I NEED IT BY TOMORROW SO GET ON IT.

YOU DON'T WANT MUCH, DO YOU? MAYBE IN BETWEEN MAKING TIME WITH THIS SONIA WOMAN YOU COULD GIVE NATE OTTOLINE A CALL? HE KNOWS THE MUSIC SCENE INSIDE OUT.

I'M WAY AHEAD OF YOU. HE AND HIS BOYFRIEND, RONNIE, ARE HELPING ME HAVE A PRIVATE, UNLISTED PHONE PUT IN SONIA'S SUITE TOMORROW.

YOU'RE GETTING A NEW PHONE IN 24 HOURS? HOW'D YOU MANAGE THAT?

PULL. WHAT ELSE?

PULL WITH PAPA BELL! YOU NEVER CEASE TO AMAZE ME, KEREMOS.

NOW, IF YOU'LL EXCUSE ME, I HAVE TO GO PAY A VISIT TO AN OLD FRIEND. THE HOUSE DICK OVER AT THE IMPERIAL PALACE HAPPENS TO OWE ME A FAVOUR.

IMPERIAL PALACE HOTEL.

I'D LIKE TO SEE CHESTER MARTIN, PLEASE.

THE HOUSE DETECTIVE? IS EVERYTHING OKAY?

OH YES, JUST AN OLD FRIEND.

DIDN'T TAKE YOU LONG TO COME CASHING IN.

GOOD TO SEE YOU TOO, CHES.

THERE WAS A MAN HANGING AROUND THIS AFTERNOON. HE USED THE HOUSE PHONE TO CALL THE DEERFIELD SUITE. DUNNO WHO HE SPOKE TO, BUT I HAPPENED TO OVERHEAR HIS END OF THE CONVERSATION. INTERESTED?

HAPPENED TO OVERHEAR?

I SAW YOU HEAD UP TO MS. DEERFIELD'S SUITE THIS MORNING. FIGURED IT MIGHT PAY OFF. NAME WAS WALT. HE MADE A DATE FOR SOMEONE TO MEET HIM AT HIS PLACE BETWEEN 2 AND 4 A.M. STRANGE TIME, EH?

OK, THAT'S WORTH A DRINK.

ONLY A DRINK? WHAT'S IT GONNA TAKE TO GET OUTTA HOCK WITH YOU? YOU KNOW WHAT, DON'T ANSWER. I CAN GUESS.

KEEP YOUR EARS OPEN, PAL.

ANYTHING TO HELP A FELLOW GUMSHOE.

15

OH, HERE SHE IS NOW!

HELEN, I'D LIKE YOU TO MEET TWO OF MY NEAREST AND DEAREST. THIS IS MY AGENT AND FRIEND, BETTY GRELICK.

AND I'M LEW DAVIES, SONIA'S CHIEF GOFER AND BOTTLE WASHER. SOMETIMES I'M EVEN HER VOCAL COACH AND ARRANGER. HA HA!

PLEASURE TO MEET YOU BOTH.

BETTY HERE WAS JUST SUGGESTING A BIT OF MONEY COULD BE SAVED BY MOVING IN SONIA'S UNCLE KARL FOR PROTECTION.

NOW, LEW, IT WASN'T AS RUDE AS ALL THAT. I WAS JUST SAYING THAT HAVING FAMILY MOVE INTO HER APARTMENT WOULD BE A BIT MORE... APPROPRIATE.

BETTY, I ADORE YOU, BUT MY DECISION IS FINAL. I FEEL SAFEST WITH HELEN.

YOU JUST MET HER THIS—

I DON'T WANT TO HEAR ANOTHER WORD ABOUT UNCLE KARL.

ALLOW ME TO HELP YOU WITH YOUR THINGS WHILE THESE TWO SORT OUT THEIR LITTLE QUARREL.

I'M FINE TO CARRY MY OWN BAG, BUT I'M HAPPY TO HAVE YOU SHOW ME TO MY ROOM.

IS THAT PRETTY TYPICAL OF THE BETTY/SONIA DYNAMIC?

HEH. YES. THEY'RE CLOSER THAN SISTERS.

WELL, I'LL LET YOU GET SETTLED.

OH! ONE THING. I ASSUME YOU'LL NEED SOME TIME TO NOT BE ON BODYGUARD WATCH SO THAT YOU CAN DO SOME, UH, DETECTING?

YES...

HERE'S SONIA'S REHEARSAL SCHEDULE. ALL THE TIMES SHE'LL BE WITH ME AND THE BAND, SAFE AND SOUND IN THE STUDIO. I THOUGHT IT MIGHT COME IN HANDY.

THANK YOU. IT'LL BE NICE TO HAVE SOME HELP MAKING SURE SHE'S NOT ALONE.

=SIGH= OTHER THAN TONIGHT...

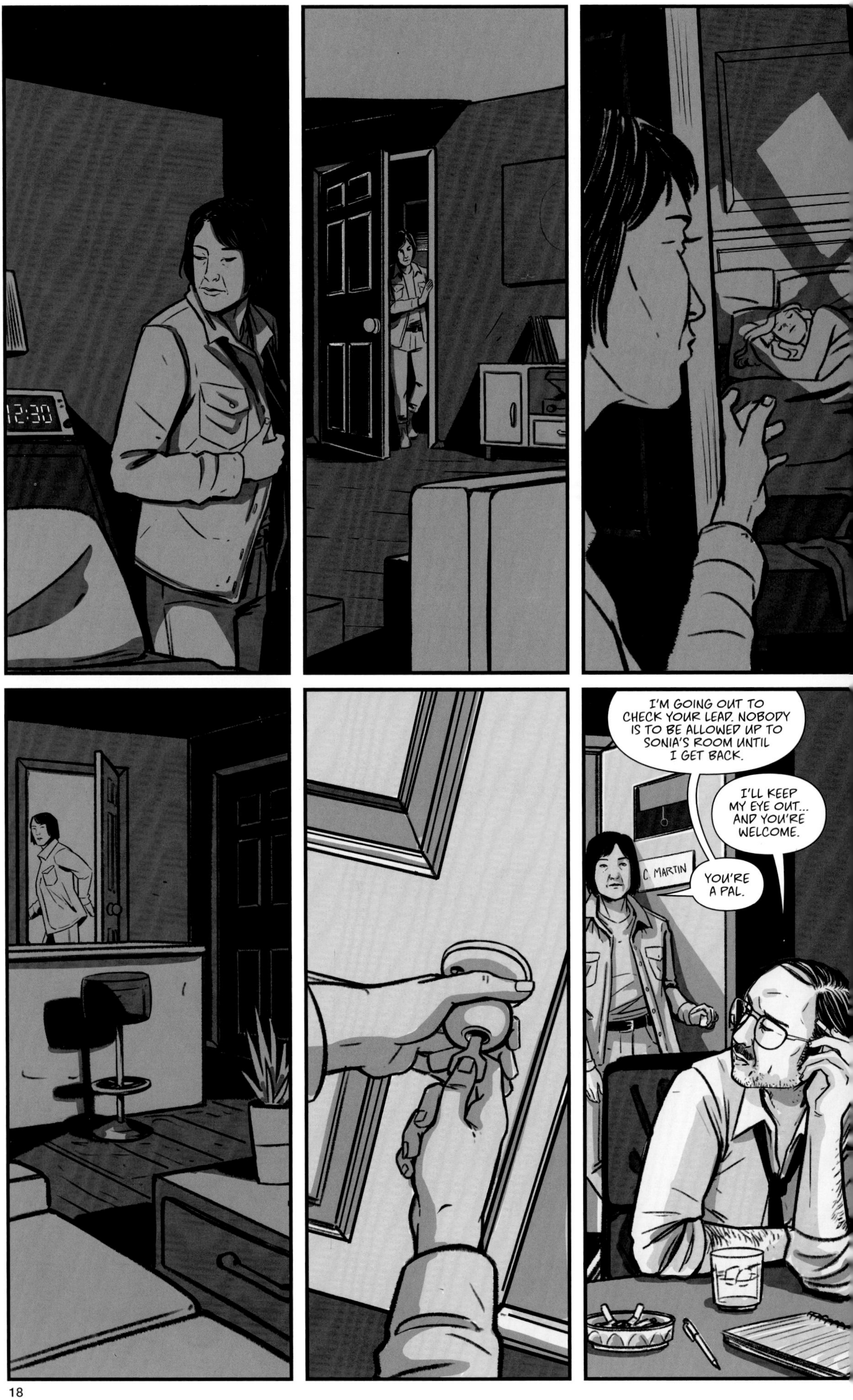
12:30
I'M GOING OUT TO CHECK YOUR LEAD. NOBODY IS TO BE ALLOWED UP TO SONIA'S ROOM UNTIL I GET BACK.
C. MARTIN
YOU'RE A PAL.
I'LL KEEP MY EYE OUT... AND YOU'RE WELCOME.

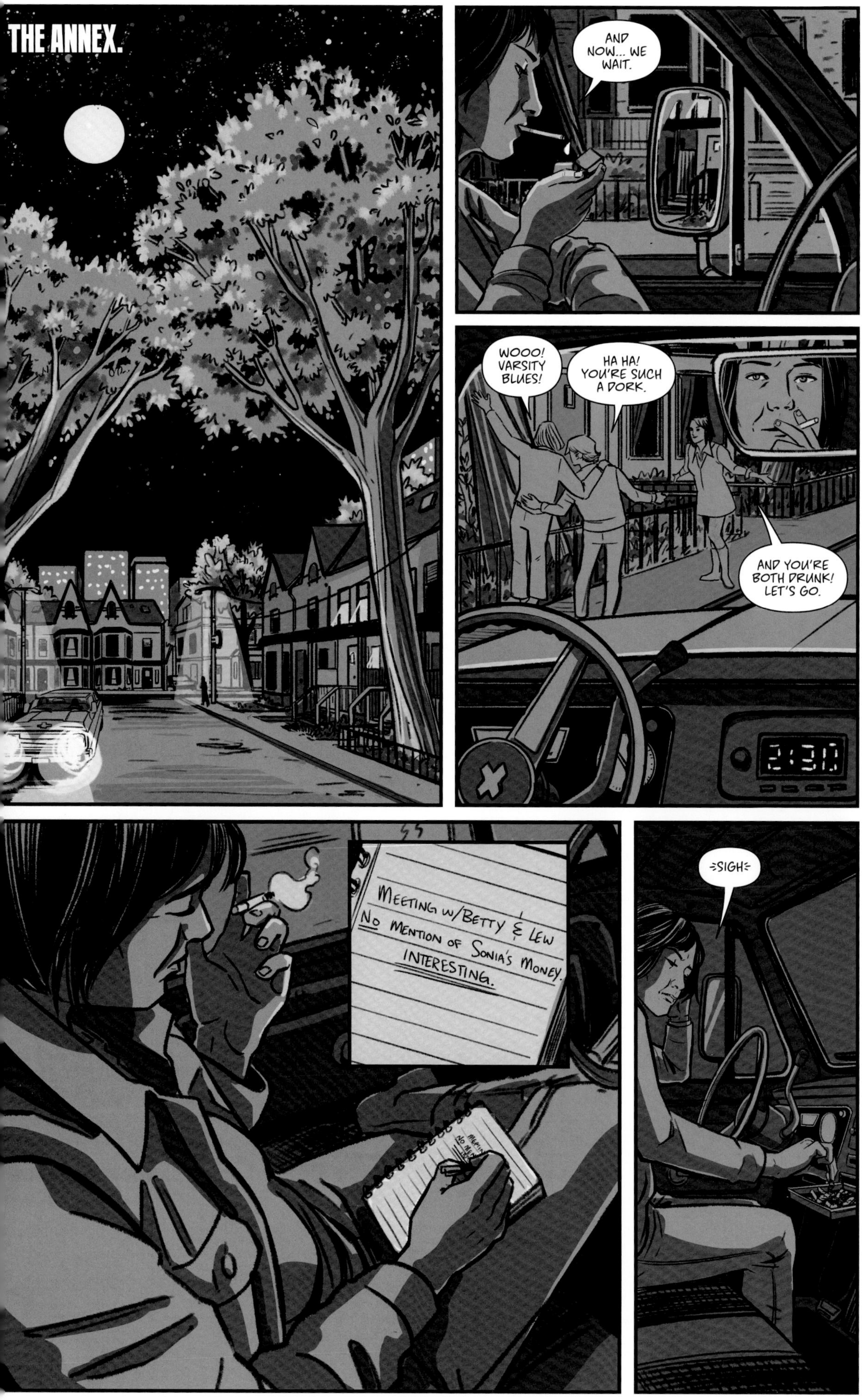
THE ANNEX.
AND NOW... WE WAIT.
WOOO! VARSITY BLUES!
HA HA! YOU'RE SUCH A DORK.
AND YOU'RE BOTH DRUNK! LET'S GO.
2:30
MEETING w/BETTY & LEW
NO MENTION OF SONIA'S MONEY.
INTERESTING.
=SIGH=

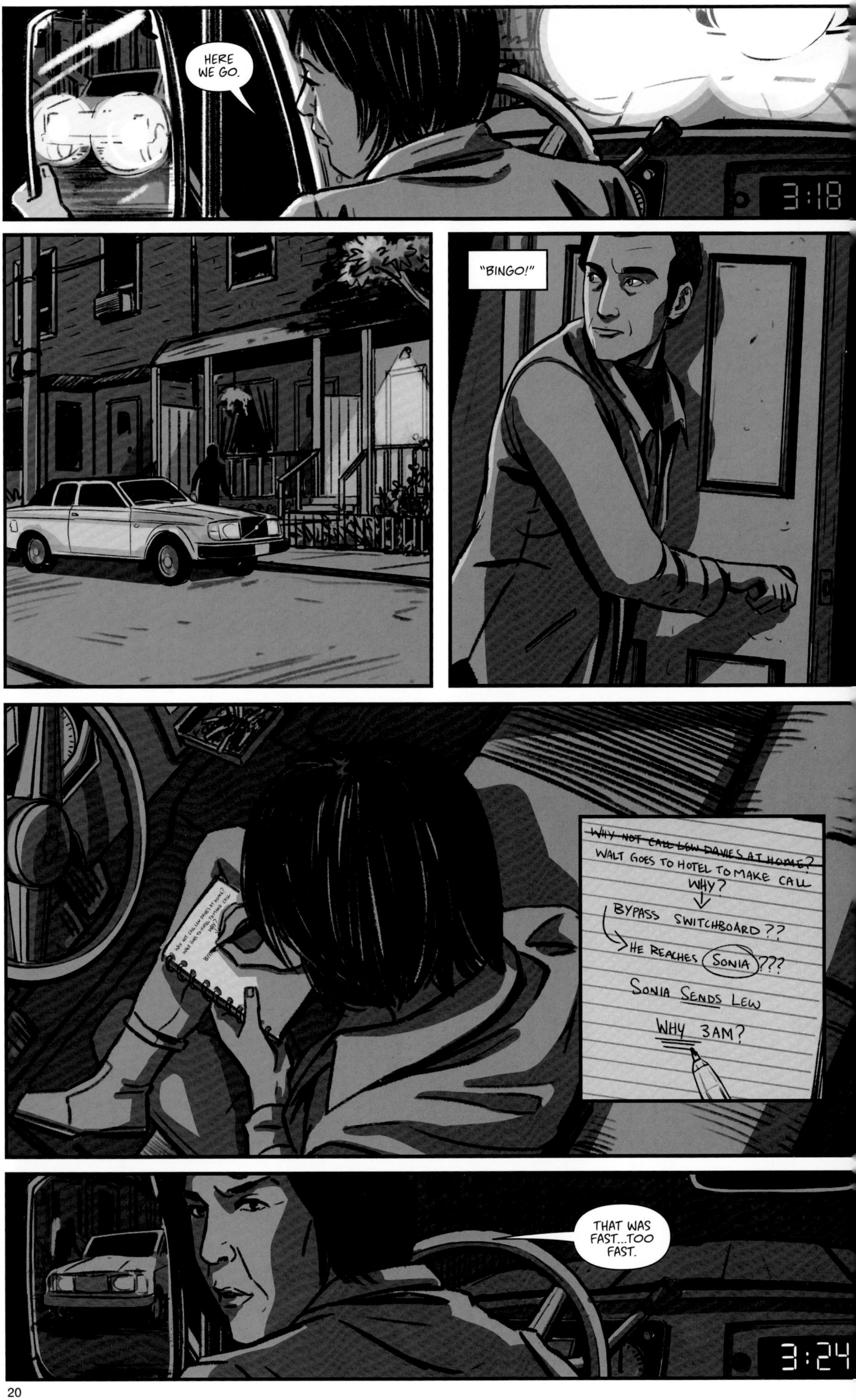
HERE WE GO.
3:18
"BINGO!"
WHY NOT CALL LEW DAVIES AT HOME?
WALT GOES TO HOTEL TO MAKE CALL
WHY?
BYPASS SWITCHBOARD??
HE REACHES SONIA???
SONIA SENDS LEW
WHY 3AM?
THAT WAS FAST...TOO FAST.
3:24

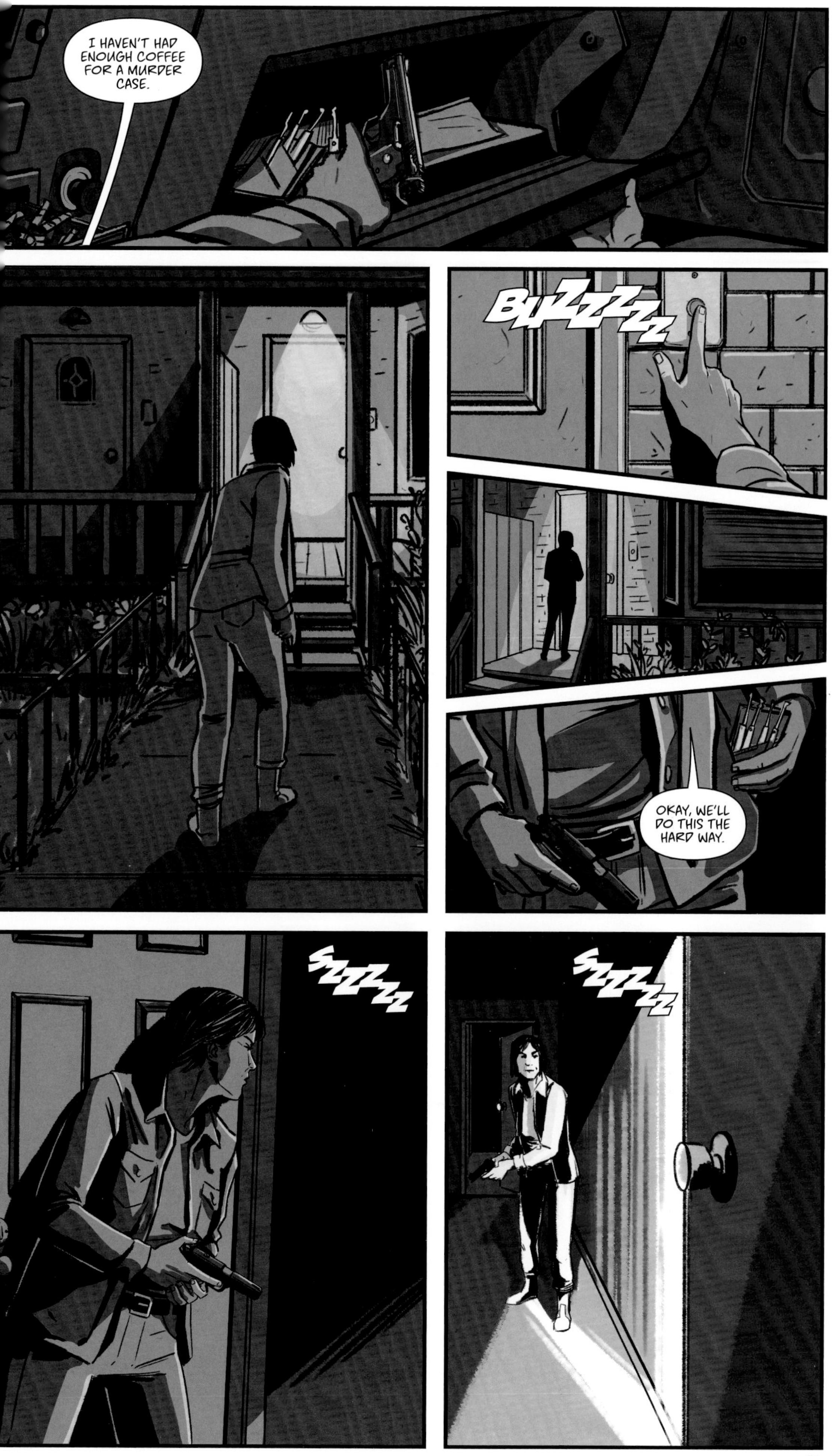
I HAVEN'T HAD ENOUGH COFFEE FOR A MURDER CASE.
BUZZZZZ
OKAY, WE'LL DO THIS THE HARD WAY.
SZZZZZ
SZZZZZ

CLICK

COME BACK FOR A BITE TO EAT?

OH! I THOUGHT YOU WERE... SOMEONE ELSE.

LEW LEFT. YOU MUST BE WALTER.

AND YOU'RE HELEN KEREMOS. HOW DO YA TAKE YOUR COFFEE?

BLACK.

I'VE A LOT ABOUT YOU.

I WISH I'D HEARD A LITTLE MORE ABOUT YOU.

OH, AT YOUR SERVICE. IT'S THE LEAST I CAN DO AFTER YOU SO GRACIOUSLY BROKE INTO MY HOME IN THE MIDDLE OF THE NIGHT.

I WOULDA KNOCKED FIRST, BUT I WASN'T SURE YOU'D HAVE A PULSE.

HAHAHAHA! LEW DAVIES HAVING THE BACKBONE TO KILL A MAN? THAT IS RICH.

NEXT TIME I'LL BE SURE NOT TO CHECK ON YOU.

HA! ALREADY GUARANTEEING A NEXT TIME. SO, SINCE YOU'RE HERE, WHAT WOULD YOU LIKE TO KNOW?

HOW WAS YOUR MARRIAGE TO SONIA?

I WAS GOOD AT IT. SHE WASN'T.

HMMM... MIND IF I GET MYSELF A LITTLE MORE COFFEE?

HERE, I'LL GET IT FOR YOU.

OH NO. I'VE BEEN ENOUGH OF AN INTRUSION...

HELP YOURSELF.

LET ME GET THAT OUT OF YOUR WAY. I'D HATE TO DAMAGE THE GOODS.

OH, ARE YOU SELLING THIS? I MIGHT HAVE TO BUY IT. IT'S A FAVOURITE OF MINE... I LOVE THE THRILL OF THE CHASE.

23

IT SEEMS YOU DO TOO.

SO, LEW WAS PAYING YOU OFF... FOR SONIA.

VERY GOOD. I SUPPOSE NOW YOU THINK I'M THE PHANTOM CALLER.

AT THE VERY LEAST, YOU'RE THE MAN WHO DIDN'T WANT ME TO KNOW HE'S BLACKMAILING MY CLIENT.

I HAVE NO INTEREST IN HARMING MY EX-WIFE. CERTAINLY NOT FOR A MEASLY $500. WHAT MOTIVE WOULD I HAVE?

I CAN THINK OF A FEW: REVENGE FOR LEAVING YOU, SHOWING YOU STILL HAVE POWER OVER HER LIFE, STICKING IT TO SEDGWICK AND HIS BOYS...

$500 ISN'T MUCH, BUT TEN MINUTES WITH YOU TELLS ME TAKING YOUR TIME TO TOY WITH SONIA WOULD CERTAINLY BE YOUR STYLE.

THIS IS AN **UNSOLICITED** GIFT. FOR OLD TIME'S SAKE. ASK SONIA.

I INTEND TO.

THAT CHEQUE CAME FROM THE MILLION DOLLAR ACCOUNT, BY THE WAY. SONIA DEPOSITED IT ALL SO NO ONE ELSE COULD GET THEIR MITTS ON IT!

YOU DON'T KNOW AS MUCH AS YOU THINK!

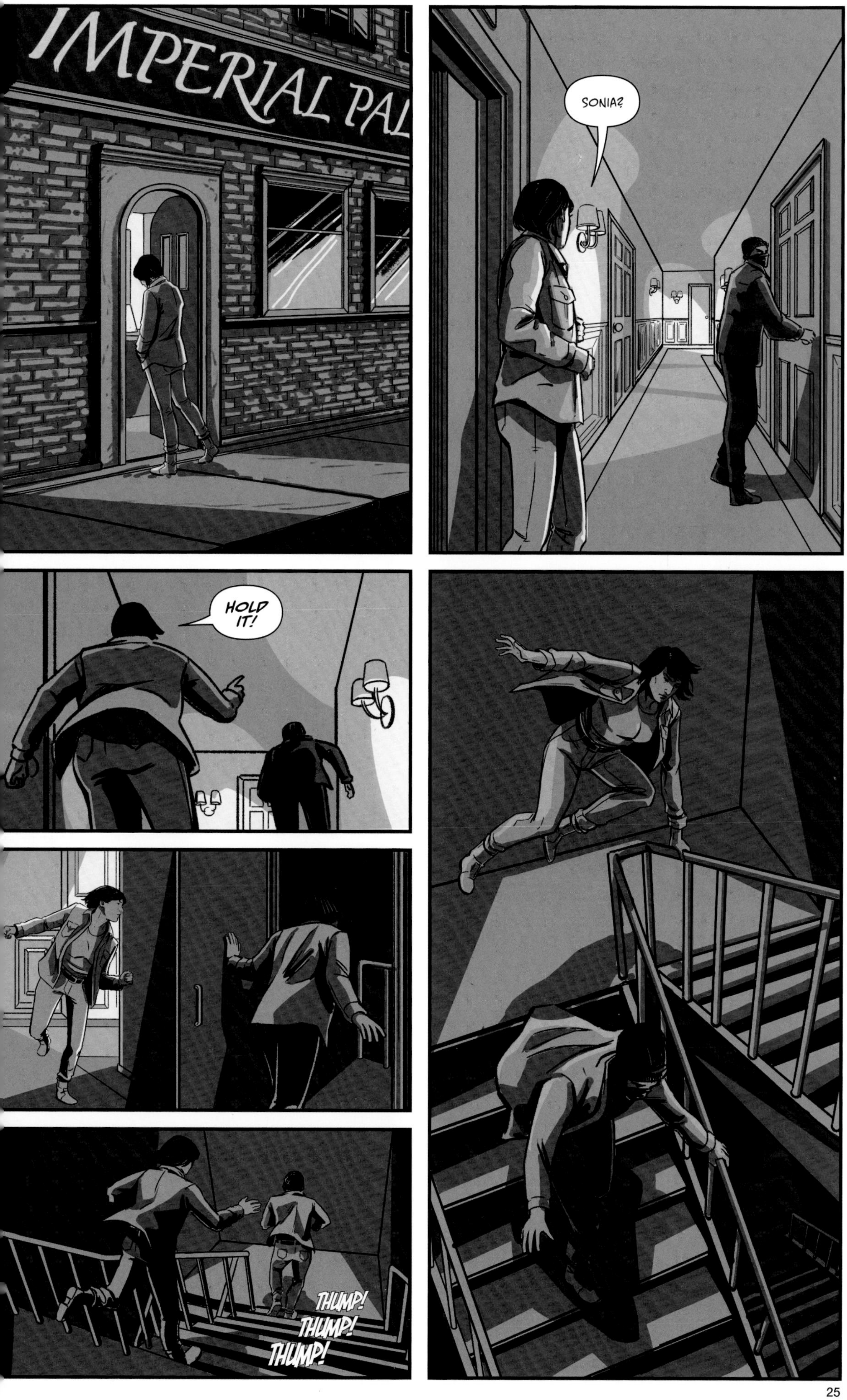
IMPERIAL PAL
SONIA?
HOLD IT!
THUMP!
THUMP!
THUMP!

THWACK!

BAM!

OOOF!

THUMP!
THUMP!

UNNNFFF!

CLUNK

SHIT.

I THOUGHT YOUR JOB WAS TO PROTECT ME, NOT LEAVE ME ALONE FOR HALF THE NIGHT.

YOU HIRED ME TO INVESTIGATE, SO I WAS INVESTIGATING.

SOMEONE TRIED TO BREAK IN.

YES. AND THEY GOT AWAY.

I SHOULD HAVE LEFT SOMEONE HERE WITH YOU. IT WON'T HAPPEN AGAIN.

I HIRED YOU BECAUSE I ALREADY HAVE ENOUGH PEOPLE DECIDING WHAT'S BEST FOR ME BEHIND MY BACK.

I'M YOUR CLIENT. I WANT TO KNOW WHAT YOU'RE DOING. UNDERSTOOD?

IT'S GOOD TO SEE YOU TAKE CHARGE. AND I AGREE. BUT TRUST GOES BOTH WAYS. YOU SENT LEW WITH A CHEQUE FOR WALT?

MY PAYING WALT IS NO BUSINESS OF YOURS. I HAVE THE MONEY, SO WHY NOT?

WHAT YOU DO ON YOUR OWN TIME IS COMPLETELY UP TO YOU.

I'M NOT HERE TO BE YOUR THERAPIST OR YOUR LOVER. WITHOUT YOUR TRUST, I CAN'T DO THE JOB I AM HERE TO DO.

JUST PROMISE NOT TO TREAT ME LIKE A CHILD. EVERYONE ELSE DOES.

THEY COULDN'T GET AWAY WITH THAT UNLESS YOU LET THEM.

I DON'T ALWAYS. SOMETIMES I DON'T TELL THEM THINGS. THEY HATE THAT.

I KNOW THE FEELING... I ASSUME DEPOSITING THE MILLION-DOLLAR WIN INTO A PRIVATE ACCOUNT WAS ONE OF THOSE THINGS YOU DIDN'T TELL THEM?

HOW'D YOU FIND THAT OUT?

WALT TOLD ME. SO, NOW THAT WE'VE DETERMINED IT'S YOUR MONEY TO SPEND AS YOU WISH... WOULD YOU BE WILLING TO PAY OFF THIS PHANTOM CALLER OF YOURS?

GIVE THIS CREEP ALL MY MONEY?

NO... JUST OFFER ENOUGH TO GET THEM TO SHOW UP FOR A DROP OFF.

IT WOULD CERTAINLY GIVE ARTHUR A HEART ATTACK.

I DON'T GIVE A RAT'S ASS ABOUT SEDGWICK'S HEALTH.

FORGET THE RULES. I NEED CARDS TO PLAY AND DOLLARS ARE ACES.

SO, ARE YOU READY TO TRUST THIS STRANGER?

ALRIGHT. DAMN ARTHUR ANYWAY. WHAT YOU'RE SAYING MAKES SENSE. I'LL OFFER A PAY-OFF THE NEXT TIME THIS WEASEL CALLS.

NOW HOW ABOUT A NIGHTCAP?

WISH I COULD...

ANOTHER TIME THEN.

I'M SO PROUD YOU KEPT THINGS PROFESSIONAL.

WELL, I TRY NOT TO MIX BUSINESS WITH PLEASURE.

AND ISN'T THAT MY ETERNAL LOSS?

YEAH, YEAH, ALEX, GIVE IT A REST.

GIVE 'EM HELL, SISTERS!

YOU BETTER BELIEVE IT!

A WOMAN'S CHOICE IS A WOMAN'S VOICE

SISTERS of the WORLD UNITE

WAGE FOR HOUSEW

WOMEN'S LIBERATION

EQUAL PAY FOR UAL WORK

MY BODY MY CHOICE

WOMEN AGAINST VIOLENCE AGAINST WOMEN

NOT THE CHURCH, NOT THE STATE, WOMEN MUST CONTROL OUR FATE!

SISTERHOOD IS POWERFUL

IF WE WEREN'T ON OUR WAY TO MEET BETTY GRELICK, I'D SAY WE SHOULD JOIN THEM.

THIS THE PLACE?

LORRAINE

YEP. GOTTA HAND IT TO BETTY: IT'S EXPENSIVE ENOUGH TO NOT INSULT US, BUT UNFASHIONABLE ENOUGH THAT SHE WON'T RUN INTO ANY HIGH-SOCIETY FRIENDS.

BETTY, I'M GLAD YOU CHOSE THIS PLACE. THIS QUICHE IS JUST DIVINE.

IT'S BEEN SO LOVELY TO MEET YOU, ALEX. I DIDN'T EXPECT HELEN TO HAVE SUCH A NICE... WELL, I MEAN, ISN'T IT NICE WHEN CLOSE FRIENDS CAN ALSO WORK WELL WITH ONE ANOTHER?

A BIT LIKE YOU AND SONIA?

WELL, YES... A BIT. I GOT SONIA HER VERY FIRST BOOKING AND THEN OVER TIME... WE BECAME... CLOSER.

I UNDERSTAND.

DO YOU? IF I SAY ANYTHING ABOUT ANY OF IT, HER MEN, HER CAREER... IT SOUNDS LIKE SOUR GRAPES. AS IT IS, I CAN'T WALK INTO A ROOM WITHOUT THE LAWYERS TREATING ME LIKE A JEALOUS BITCH.

OH HONEY, WE'VE ALL BEEN THERE.

SURE, BUT NOW THERE'S THIS MILLION DOLLARS... IT'S ALL SO HORRIBLE!

A MILLION DOLLARS AIN'T SO HORRIBLE, BUT I GET THE PICTURE. YOU CAN'T WIN.

AND NOW SHE'S HIRED YOU, AND I SIT HERE WONDERING IF THAT'S A GOOD THING OR NOT.

WELL, I GUESS THAT ALL DEPENDS ON POINT OF VIEW. THE PHANTOM CALLER WOULD CERTAINLY SEE HIRING ME AS A BAD THING...

YOU'RE NOT SUGGESTING I—

I'M NOT SUGGESTING ANYTHING. YOU'RE NOT SURE IT'S GOOD THAT I WANT TO GET TO THE BOTTOM OF THIS?

NO! I DIDN'T MEAN TO IMPLY—I JUST—WE ALL KNOW IT'S PROBABLY WALT PLAYING ONE OF HIS SILLY GAMES. HE WOULDN'T HURT SONIA FOR REAL. HE'LL GET BORED AND MOVE ON.

YOU HOPE! SHIT, I CAN'T BELIEVE IT. SOME FRIEND YOU ARE. WE DON'T EVEN KNOW IT IS WALT. AND WHAT ABOUT SEDGWICK AND BONO?

OH BEN BONO JUST USES MONEY AS LEVERAGE TO GET SONIA TO MARRY HIM SO HE CAN "LOOK AFTER HER." BUT HOW DO YOU SEE IT?

I PAID WALT A LITTLE VISIT LAST NIGHT. I THINK IT'LL SOON BE POSSIBLE TO DETERMINE WHETHER HE'S THE PHANTOM CALLER OR NOT.

YOU DID?! HOW DID... I MEAN... SO YOU THINK NOW HE'LL EITHER STOP, OR—GO EVEN FURTHER?

EXACTLY.

ONE LAST QUESTION: DO YOU THINK LEW DAVIES IS WALT'S INSIDE MAN?

LEW?! ABSOLUTELY NOT. FOR THE LONGEST TIME IT WAS JUST THE THREE OF US. ME, SONIA, AND LEW. I'D TRUST HIM WITH MY LIFE... AND SONIA'S.

WHAT DO YOU THINK?

I DUNNO WHAT HER THERAPIST WOULD SAY—BUT SHE'S WORKING HARD NOT TO SEE WHAT SHE'S REALLY AFTER.

YOU MEAN SHE DOESN'T REALIZE SHE'S IN LOVE WITH SONIA.

YEAH AND IF SHE DID, IT WOULD SCARE HER SHITLESS, SO LET'S DROP IT.

EVERYONE SEEMS TO BE IN LOVE WITH SONIA.

EXCEPT SONIA.

IMPERIAL PALACE HOTEL, JARVIS STREET.

UH, EX—EXCUSE ME, HELEN, UH, MS. KEREMOS?

YOU SEEM TO HAVE ME AT A DISADVANTAGE, MR...?

HA! OH YES, EXCUSE MY LACK OF MANNERS. I'M KARL DEERFIELD. I'M, UH, SONIA'S UNCLE.

I WASN'T UNDER THE IMPRESSION SHE HAD CLOSE FAMILY.

OH, WELL, NO... SHE WOULDN'T CALL US CLOSE. I'M AFRAID I CAN BE A BIT TEDIOUS, AND WE LIVED SO FAR APART FOR SO LONG.

NO, I JUST WANTED TO DROP IN AND... ARE YOU GOING UP, BY ANY CHANCE?

NO, NOT ANYMORE. I THINK I'LL JUST RELAX IN THE LOBBY FOR A BIT.

...ON SECOND THOUGHT, IT SUITS YOU.

BY ALL MEANS, DON'T LET ME STOP YOU FROM PAYING YOUR VISIT.

OH, NO. I... UH, I'LL WAIT WITH YOU....

SO YOU'RE A PRIVATE DETECTIVE? THAT'S A STRANGE JOB FOR A YOUNG LADY.

IS IT?

YES, LEW, I THINK THAT WOULD BE JUST—

...

I'VE TOLD YOU NEVER TO COME HERE.

OH... AHEM... I WAS HOPING WE COULD HAVE A NICE FAMILY CHAT.

LET ME WALK YOU OUT, KARL.

GOOD TO SEE YOU TOO, LEW.

NOW, NOW. I'LL WALK MYSELF OUT. I JUST WANTED TO CHECK IN AFTER MY NIECE.

YOU KNOW, SEE WHAT KIND OF PROTECTION SHE HAS IN PLACE.

SHALL I HELP YOU OUT THE DOOR?

I'M GOING! I'M GOING.

WELL, NOW YOU'VE MET ABSOLUTELY EVERYONE IN SONIA'S LIFE, HELEN.

SO, UNCLE KARL CAN'T BE TRUSTED AND HIDES BEHIND AN AIR OF HARMLESS HELPLESSNESS.

I GOT THAT IN THE FIRST FIVE MINUTES. ANYTHING ELSE I SHOULD KNOW?

HE'S NOT WELCOME HERE. THAT'S ALL YOU NEED TO KNOW FOR NOW.

JUST PARK IN ANY SPACE THAT DON'T HAVE A NAME ON IT...

UNAUTHORIZED VEHICLES WILL BE TOWED

TRI-MET Studios

HEY, HOW MANY CARS COMIN' WITH YOUR GROUP TODAY ANYWAY?

NO IDEA. I JUST KNOW ONE'S A WHITE VOLVO.

THE STAR, HUH? IMAGINE HAVIN' THAT KIND OF MONEY AND THAT'S WHAT YOU DRIVE? HEH. ARTISTS.

YOU FROM THE UNIVERSAL SOUND OUTFIT?

I'M WITH WHATEVER OUTFIT IS PRODUCING MUSIC FOR SONIA DEERFIELD.

THAT'S THE ONE. SHALL I SHOW YOU TO THE GREEN ROOM?

I'D LOVE THAT.

OH...

HOW DO YOU TAKE YOUR COFFEE?

HOT.

I KNOW YOU NEED TO KEEP AN EYE ON ME, BUT TODAY IT'S JUST THE BAND AND HONESTLY, THEY'RE FAMILY, SO JUST RELAX AND ENJOY THE SHOW!

OH, HELEN, YOU'RE HERE!

PLEASE TELL ME YOU'LL SIT IN THE BOOTH AND LISTEN! I'M JUST DYING TO KNOW WHAT YOU THINK!

I WOULDN'T HAVE LISTENED IF THEY'D TOLD MEEEEE. I'D WANT YOUUUU.... TO HOLD MEEEE.

SHE'S GOOD, ISN'T SHE?

NICE TO SEE YOU AGAIN, SEDGWICK. YES, SHE'S VERY GOOD. NOT MANY SINGERS CAN MANAGE TO SOUND INNOCENT AND WORLD-WEARY AT THE SAME TIME...

...BABY, LET YOUR LOVE CONTROL ME, I DON'T CARE WHO MAY SCOLD MEEEE...

OF COURSE, ALL THE BIG-MONEY ELECTRONICS CERTAINLY DON'T HURT THE EFFECT.

WELL, SONIA AND LEW MAKE THE CREATIVE DECISIONS. IT'S ALL OVER MY HEAD.

SO WHAT'S YOUR PART IN ALL OF THIS?

BEN BONO AND I LOOK AFTER ALL SONIA'S INTERESTS. IT'S GETTING TO BE QUITE A SUBSTANTIAL BUSINESS.

THEN I GUESS YOU KNOW EVERYONE WHO IS ON HER PAYROLL? LIKE... WALTER LAUKER?

SONIA HAS ASSURED ME THAT WALTER ISN'T GETTING ANY KIND OF—

OH, HE'S BEING PAID. I'VE SEEN THE CHEQUE. I'M NOT SURE WHY YOU ARE PRETENDING TO HAVE YOUR HANDS ON SONIA'S MONEY, BUT IT DOESN'T EXACTLY PAINT YOU IN THE BEST LIGHT.

I THINK I MISJUDGED YOU, HELEN. I HAD NO IDEA YOU'D BE SO INTERESTED IN MY AFFAIRS.

I'M INTERESTED IN MY CLIENT'S AFFAIRS.

HA! COME NOW. YOU THINK I'M AFTER SONIA FOR HER MONEY? SHE'S ONLY WON IT RECENTLY.

BEN AND I HAD BEEN WORKING WITH HER FOR MONTHS BEFORE ALL THAT. I SUPPOSE YOU THINK WE'RE THE PHANTOM CALLER AS WELL?

OH, NOT AT ALL. IF ANYTHING, I'D BET YOU FIND THE CALLER TO BE A NUISANCE... BUT I DO THINK YOU'RE UP TO SOMETHING.

YOUR JOB IS TO FIND OUT WHO THE CALLER IS. I'M A BUSY MAN. I'M AFRAID I CAN'T ALLOW FOR ANY NUISANCES.

IF YOU DON'T GET YOUR HANDS OFF ME I'LL BE A LOT MORE THAN A NUISANCE...

ENJOY THE REST OF THE SONG.

CHERRAE... THAT'S A LOVELY NAME.

OH.. HEHE, THANKS. AND YOURS?

HELEN. HELEN KEREMOS.

SO ARE YOU IN THE INDUSTRY?

I'M... INDUSTRY-ADJACENT.

OH YOU MUST BE IMPORTANT TO BE SO COY! LEMME GUESS, YOU'RE FROM UNIVERSAL? MISS DEERFIELD MUST BE EXCITED TO HAVE SO MUCH INTEREST THIS EARLY.

IS THAT UNUSUAL?

I'M SORRY, DON'T MISUNDERSTAND ME... A ROOKIE POP SINGER DOESN'T USUALLY GET THIS MUCH ATTENTION FROM A MAJOR COMPANY. YOU'RE IN THE BUSINESS. YOU UNDERSTAND.

ACTUALLY, I'M SURE YOU KNOW MORE ABOUT IT THAN I DO... I'D LOVE TO PICK YOUR BRAIN. PERHAPS OVER DINNER?

THAT SOUNDS DELIGHTFUL—

SIR! YOU CAN'T JUST—

I'M JUST HERE TO OFFER A BIT OF FAMILIAL SUPPORT!

I'M SORRY. IT SEEMS DINNER WILL HAVE TO WAIT.

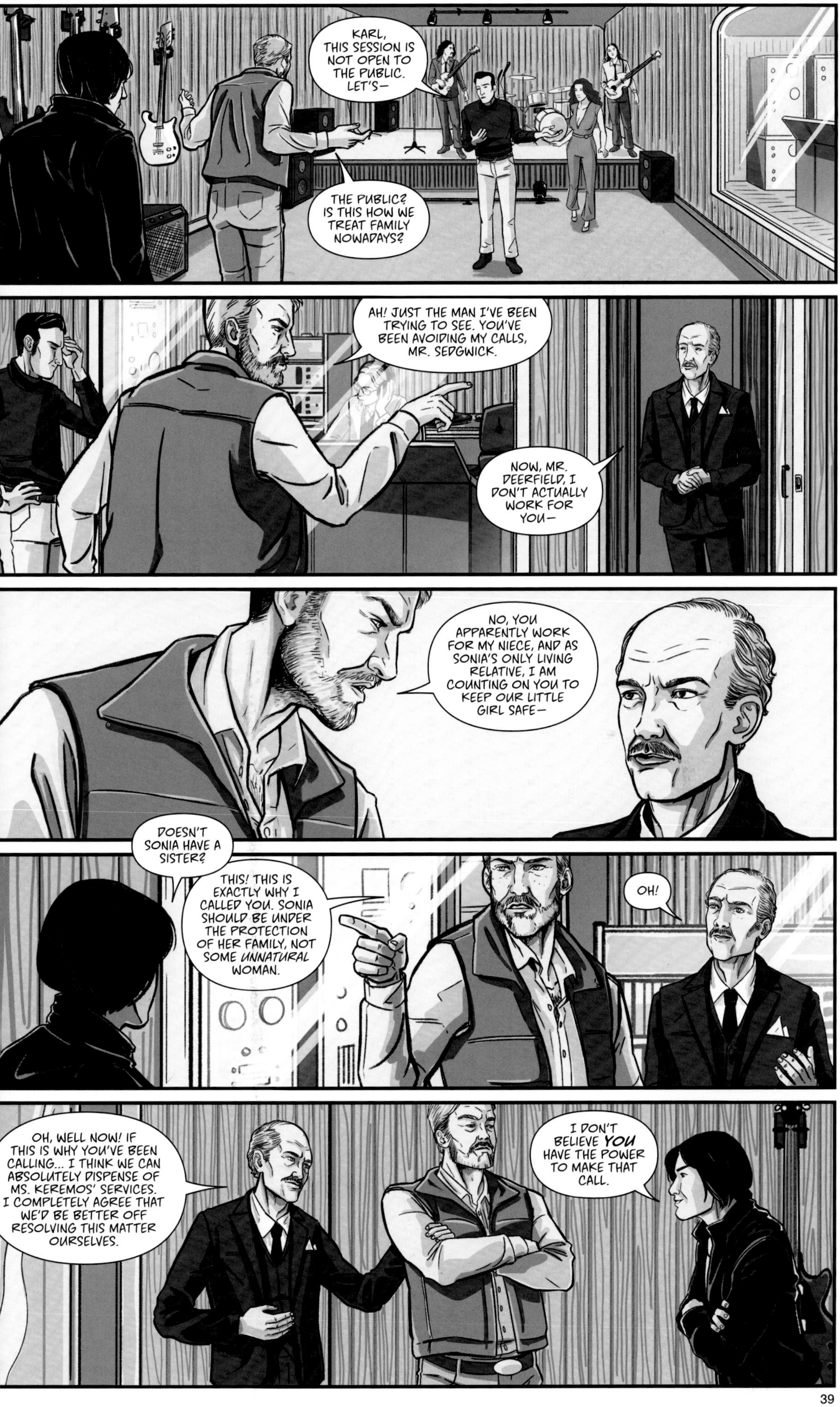
KARL, THIS SESSION IS NOT OPEN TO THE PUBLIC. LET'S—
THE PUBLIC? IS THIS HOW WE TREAT FAMILY NOWADAYS?
AH! JUST THE MAN I'VE BEEN TRYING TO SEE. YOU'VE BEEN AVOIDING MY CALLS, MR. SEDGWICK.
NOW, MR. DEERFIELD, I DON'T ACTUALLY WORK FOR YOU—
NO, YOU APPARENTLY WORK FOR MY NIECE, AND AS SONIA'S ONLY LIVING RELATIVE, I AM COUNTING ON YOU TO KEEP OUR LITTLE GIRL SAFE—
DOESN'T SONIA HAVE A SISTER?
THIS! THIS IS EXACTLY WHY I CALLED YOU. SONIA SHOULD BE UNDER THE PROTECTION OF HER FAMILY, NOT SOME *UNNATURAL* WOMAN.
OH!
OH, WELL NOW! IF THIS IS WHY YOU'VE BEEN CALLING... I THINK WE CAN ABSOLUTELY DISPENSE OF MS. KEREMOS' SERVICES. I COMPLETELY AGREE THAT WE'D BE BETTER OFF RESOLVING THIS MATTER OURSELVES.
I DON'T BELIEVE ***YOU*** HAVE THE POWER TO MAKE THAT CALL.

THAT'S RIGHT! AND I WANT YOU TO GET OUT! BOTH OF YOU!

ARTHUR, I'LL SEE YOU TOMORROW. AND UNCLE KARL, DON'T YOU DARE SHOW YOUR FACE AROUND HERE AGAIN.

HELEN STAYS AND THAT'S FINAL.

MY DEAR, YOU'RE UNDER TREMENDOUS STRAIN. WHY DON'T YOU GO ON WITH YOUR SESSION AND LET ME HANDLE THIS?

GET OUT, OR YOU WON'T BE HANDLING ANYTHING FOR ME EVER AGAIN.

WE'LL DISCUSS THE MATTER TOMORROW.

YES, WHAT A GREAT IDEA!

PACK IT UP EVERYONE. WE'LL COME BACK TOMORROW WITH FRESH VOICES.

SONIA WE'RE STILL SCHEDULED FOR—

I'M PAYING FOR THIS, LEW. THAT "WHO ARE YOU?" NUMBER NEEDS WORK ANYWAY. WE CAN LOOK OVER THE ARRANGEMENTS IN THE MORNING.

WELL, LOOK WHO DECIDED TO SHOW UP AND BE THE BOSS.

HOW ABOUT TAKING THE BOSS OUT OF HERE? DON'T YOU HAVE A BRAND NEW TRUCK?

I DO.

I'VE ALWAYS WANTED TO LEARN HOW TO DRIVE STICK.

IT'S GOOD TO SEE YOU OUT FROM UNDER SEDGWICK'S INFLUENCE. I'M IMPRESSED.

FUCK ARTHUR'S INFLUENCE! LET'S JUST DRIVE. GO GET HAMMERED SOMEWHERE. I WANT A NIGHT WHERE I DON'T HAVE TO DISCUSS THE MUSIC INDUSTRY... OR THIS DAMN BLACKMAILER.

SOUNDS GREAT TO ME.

SO... HOW DO I DRIVE THIS THING?

WHILE YOUR RIGHT FOOT WORKS THE BRAKE, PUT YOUR LEFT FOOT ON THE CLUTCH AND SHIFT THE GEARS.

LIKE THIS?

PERFECT. YOU'RE A NATURAL. NOW LET'S JUST PRACTICE TAKING IT ALL THE WAY UP TO FIFTH.

I THINK I'VE—

WWRRR

WRRRRRRRI

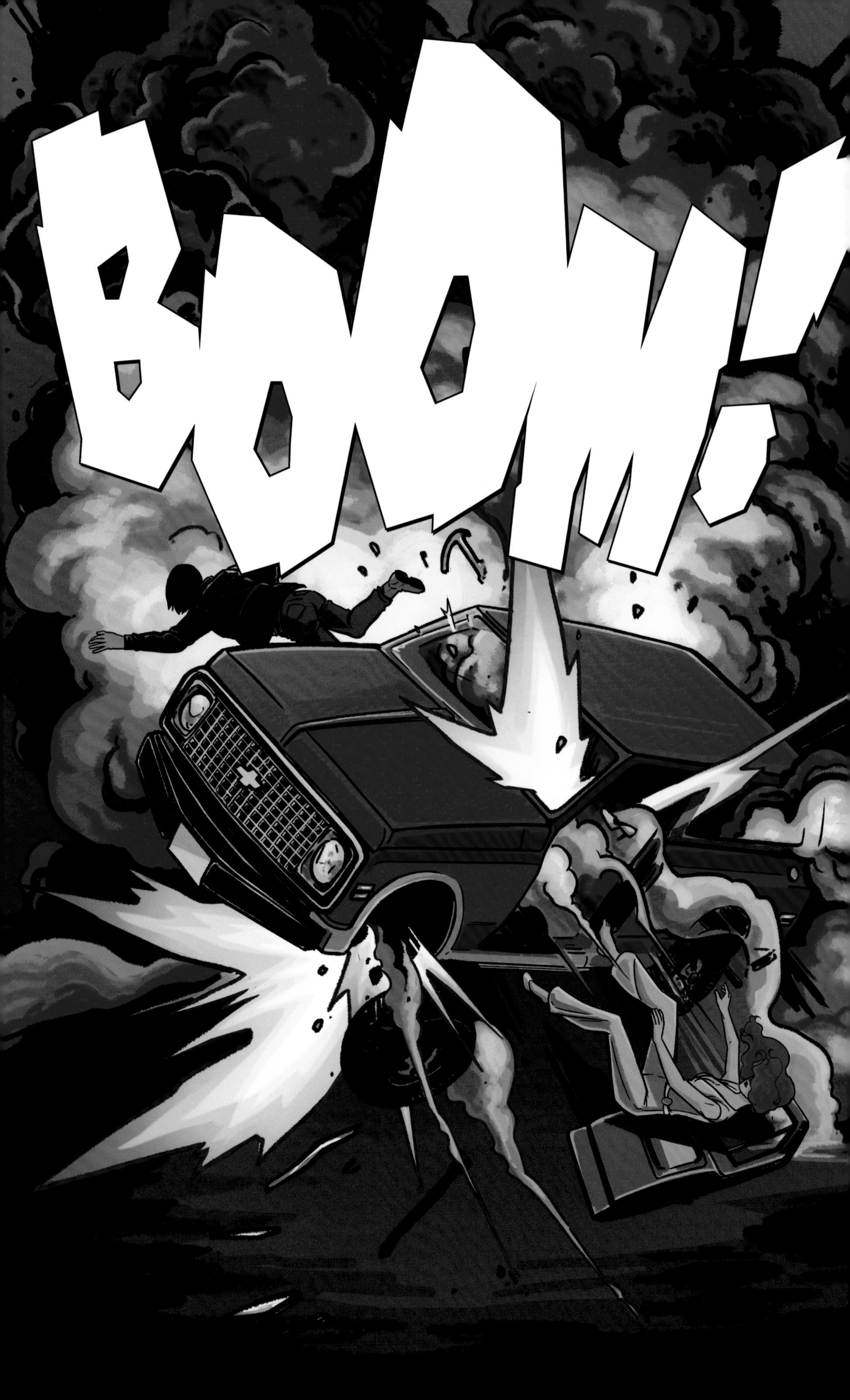
BOOM!

SHE'S OPENING HER EYES.

ALEX... NATE...

HOW YA FEELIN', KID?

WHERE'S SONIA?!

SHE'S JUST DOWN THE HALL. SHE'S NOT AWAKE YET, BUT SHE'LL BE FINE.

I HOPE IT'S OKAY I CALLED NATE. I KNEW THAT HE'D WANT TO BE HERE. THERE'S ALSO A POLICE DETECTIVE WHO WANTS TO—

GOOD. YOU'RE AWAKE. MY NAME'S DETECTIVE SERGEANT FRANCIS MALLORY. I'VE GOT A FEW QUESTIONS.

302

YOU OKAY, HELEN? BECAUSE IF YOU AREN'T READY TO TALK TO THE MAN, YOU SURE DON'T HAVE TO...

I'LL BE FINE. THANKS, NATE.

WE'LL BE RIGHT OUTSIDE.

VERY PROTECTIVE ASSOCIATES YOU HAVE THERE.

VERY CARING FRIENDS. BUT LET'S CUT TO THE CHASE. WHO DO YA LIKE FOR THE BOMBING?

301

I UNDERSTAND YOU'VE BEEN DOING SOME P.I. WORK FOR SONIA DEERFIELD. YOU A BODYGUARD TOO?

WE FOUND AN S&W LUGER IN THE WRECKAGE.

YOU ALSO FOUND A LICENSE FOR IT IN MY WALLET. LET'S CUT THE CRAP. I'VE BEEN WORKING ON THIS CASE LONGER THAN YOU. YOU CAN TREAT ME LIKE A SUSPECT OR WE CAN HELP EACH OTHER.

BOMB SQUAD FIGURES A SMALL EXPLOSIVE CHARGE WAS PLACED BETWEEN THE ENGINE BLOCK AND THE FIREWALL.

SO IT WAS PROBABLY THE CLUTCH MOVEMENT THAT COMPLETED THE CIRCUIT.

YOU SURE KNOW YOUR WAY AROUND A HOMEMADE BOMB...

NOT MY FIRST BRUSH WITH DEATH.

YOU THINK YOU'RE THE INTENDED VICTIM?

THERE'S NO WAY ANYONE COULD HAVE KNOWN SONIA WAS GOING TO BE IN MY TRUCK.

HAVE YOU SPOKEN WITH ARTHUR SEDGWICK?

HE AND HIS ASSOCIATE, BENJAMIN BONO, GAVE THEIR STATEMENTS ALREADY.

I BET THEY DID. AND BECAUSE SEDGWICK HAS LOTS OF JUICE IN THIS TOWN YOU HAVE TO SPEND YOUR TIME INVESTIGATING ME. DID ANYONE MENTION WALTER LAUKER?

THEY ALL DID.

AH, WELL, FOR MY MONEY HE'S CLEAN.

WE'LL SEE. HOW ABOUT YOUR FRIENDS OUT THERE?

THEY'RE OLD FRIENDS WHO WEREN'T THERE. YOU CAN SEND THEM IN ON YOUR WAY OUT... UNLESS YOU'D RATHER I CALL UP THE NEWSPAPERS TO COMPLAIN ABOUT BEING FINGERPRINTED WHILE I WAS UNCONSCIOUS. NOT QUITE KOSHER, HUH?

H—

SPARE THE EXCUSES. I GET IT. YOU WERE IN A HURRY TO IDENTIFY ME. CLOSE THE DOOR ON YOUR WAY OUT.

HELP ME UP.

HELEN, TAKE IT EASY. YOU'VE ONLY BEEN CONSCIOUS FOR TWENTY MINUTES!

YEAH, WHAT TOOK YOU SO LONG?

HA! GETTING LAZY IN MY MIDDLE AGE, I GUESS. I'M GONNA NEED YOU TWO TO START TRACKING SEDGWICK AND BONO. I'VE ENSURED DETECTIVE MALLORY WILL KEEP TABS ON WALTER.

HOW'D YA DO THAT?

BY SAYING I THINK HE'S INNOCENT.

YOU SHOULDN'T BE UP YET!

OH I KNOW, BUT I NEEDED A CHANGE OF SCENERY.

SEE? THAT'S BETTER ALREADY.

OH... WELL...

SO, HOW'S THE COFFEE AROUND HERE? THE STUFF THEY SERVE IN THE ROOMS IS AWFUL. ANY CHANCE YOU HAVE SOMETHING THAT'S A LITTLE... TASTIER?

YOU KNOW, I REALLY SHOULDN'T...

DON'T WORRY ABOUT IT. I WOULDN'T WANT TO GET YOU IN TROUBLE. AND HONESTLY, JUST TALKING TO YOU IS PERKING ME RIGHT UP.

OH... WAIT RIGHT HERE.

VISITORS LOG

PATIENT: DEERFIELD, SONIA

Visitor Name	TIME IN	TIME OUT	Signature
A. Sedgwick	9:30	9:45	Willer Sedgwick
Ben Bono	9:40	10:05	Ben Bono
Betty Grelick	10:30	11:00	Betty Grelick
Lew Davies	10:30	11:00	Lew Davies

DIRECTORY

JUST DON'T TELL ANYONE.

YOUR SECRET IS SAFE WITH ME.

WELL, I DIDN'T EXPECT YOU UP SO SOON.

IT SEEMS WE'RE STUCK WITH EACH OTHER. INCIDENTALLY, DO YOU KNOW WHERE KARL DEERFIELD IS? EVERYONE ELSE HAS BEEN IN TO VISIT SONIA, BUT NO SIGN OF UNCLE KARL.

HE'S MOVING HIS THINGS INTO SONIA'S APARTMENT SO SOMEONE CAN KEEP A PROPER EYE ON HER. SHAME THERE WON'T BE ANY ROOM FOR YOU. I'M SURE HE'LL BE OVER PRESENTLY TO LET HER KNOW.

YOU MEAN SHE HASN'T BEEN CONSULTED?

WELL, I ONLY JUST GOT WORD SHE'S EVEN AWAKE. AS HER LAWYER IT'S MY DUTY TO LOOK OUT FOR HER WHEN SHE'S INCAPACITATED.

CAREFUL, SEDGWICK, YOU'RE OVERESTIMATING YOUR PULL.

WE'LL SEE, MS. KEREMOS.

IT'S GOOD TO SEE YOU UP.

HELEN! I'M SO GLAD YOU'RE OKAY! OH, I MUST LOOK A FRIGHT. WOULD YOU COMB MY HAIR?

IS IT STRANGE THAT I AM HAPPIER HERE, IN THE HOSPITAL, THAN I HAVE BEEN FOR MONTHS? IT'S THE FIRST TIME IN SO LONG THAT NO ONE WANTS ANYTHING FROM ME.

THERE ARE BETTER WAYS TO GET A VACATION.

HA HA! TRUE.

47

THIS IS SO LOVELY, THANK YOU. ÷SIGH÷ HOW DO I GET OUT OF THE MESS THAT IS MY LIFE?

DON'T GET MORBID ON ME. WE'LL FIGURE OUT WHO'S BEHIND THIS. THAT BOMB SUGGESTS DESPERATION AND DESPERATE PEOPLE, GET SLOPPY.

EVEN AFTER THE BOMB... YOU STILL THINK IT'S SOMEONE CLOSE TO YOU?

YES.

AND WHOEVER IT IS WANTS ME OUT OF THE PICTURE ONE WAY OR ANOTHER. RIGHT NOW YOUR UNCLE KARL IS TRYING TO MOVE INTO YOUR APARTMENT.

OH MY GOD! NO! NO! NO! HE CAN'T! HELEN! NO!

SONIA, AS LONG AS I'M AROUND, NO ONE IS GOING TO DO ANYTHING YOU DON'T WANT THEM TO.

BUT YOU'VE GOTTA BE STRAIGHT WITH ME. THAT KIND OF REACTION TELLS ME THIS ISN'T ABOUT UNCLE KARL BEING AN ANNOYING ROOMMATE.

I WAS EIGHT WHEN IT STARTED.

"MY MOTHER ADORED HIM. MY FATHER WAS IN AWE OF HIM.

"I WAS A GOOD GIRL. I DIDN'T WANT TO DISAPPOINT MY PARENTS. I KNEW THEY'D BE UPSET IF I TOLD THEM WHAT HE WAS DOING TO ME, SO I DIDN'T.

"IT WAS MY LITTLE SISTER WHO BLEW THE LID OFF THE WHOLE THING. SHE WAS JEALOUS OF THE TOYS AND ATTENTION HE GAVE ME. EVENTUALLY SHE SAW SOMETHING UNTOWARD AND TOLD MY MOTHER..."

I'M GLAD SHE DID.

MY MOTHER WOULDN'T BELIEVE IT AT FIRST... AND THEN SHE BLAMED ME. KARL SAID HE COULDN'T HELP HIMSELF... AND SHE ADORED HIM, SO... SOMEHOW I WAS AN EIGHT-YEAR-OLD TEMPTRESS.

I'M SO SORRY.

"I LOST MY MOTHER THAT DAY. WHEN I WAS FOURTEEN, I GOT ENOUGH BUS FARE TO MAKE IT TO TORONTO AND I'VE NEVER LOOKED BACK."

49

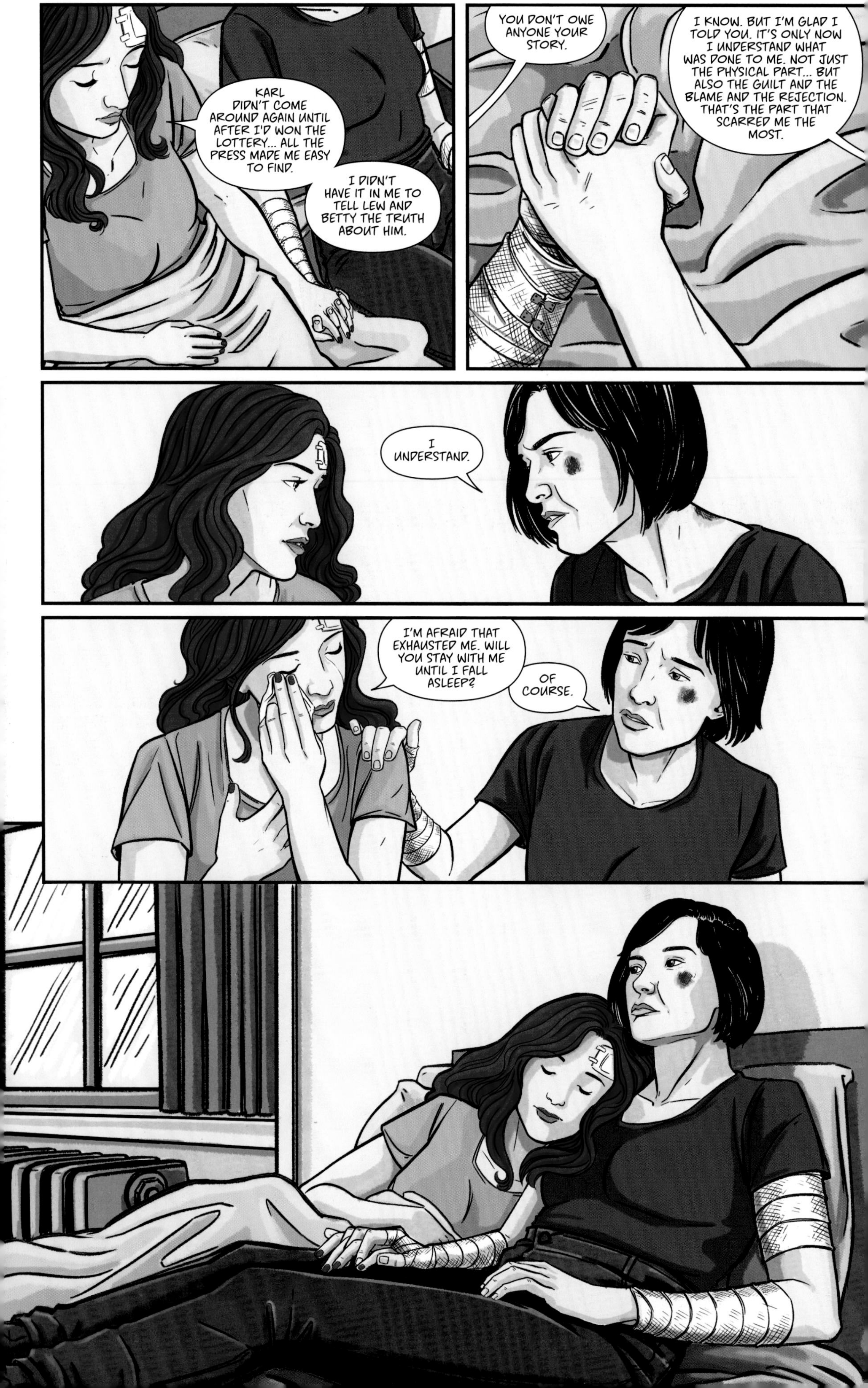
KARL DIDN'T COME AROUND AGAIN UNTIL AFTER I'D WON THE LOTTERY... ALL THE PRESS MADE ME EASY TO FIND.
I DIDN'T HAVE IT IN ME TO TELL LEW AND BETTY THE TRUTH ABOUT HIM.
YOU DON'T OWE ANYONE YOUR STORY.
I KNOW. BUT I'M GLAD I TOLD YOU. IT'S ONLY NOW I UNDERSTAND WHAT WAS DONE TO ME. NOT JUST THE PHYSICAL PART... BUT ALSO THE GUILT AND THE BLAME AND THE REJECTION. THAT'S THE PART THAT SCARRED ME THE MOST.
I UNDERSTAND.
I'M AFRAID THAT EXHAUSTED ME. WILL YOU STAY WITH ME UNTIL I FALL ASLEEP?
OF COURSE.

SONIA, MEET MY TWO CLOSEST FRIENDS AND ASSOCIATES: ALEX EDWARDS AND NATE OTTOLINE.

OH HELLO! IT'S SO NICE TO FINALLY MEET YOU.

PLEASURE.

WE'VE HEARD NOTHING BUT LOVELY THINGS ABOUT YOU.

I THINK WE'VE COME UP WITH A PLAN TO DRAW OUT THE BLACKMAILER. IT'S A LITTLE RISKY...

I TRUST YOU.

GREAT. LET'S SET A TRAP FOR THIS BLACKMAILING BASTARD.

"FIRST, SONIA, YOU'LL CHECK OUT OF THE HOSPITAL AND MOVE BACK INTO YOUR HOTEL ROOM... WITHOUT KARL.

"NEXT, NEGLIGENT BODYGUARD THAT I AM... I'LL LEAVE YOU ALONE JUST LONG ENOUGH TO HAVE A LITTLE CHAT WITH OUR KEY PLAYERS: LEW DAVIES, BEN BONO, AND ARTHUR SEDGWICK. I'LL LET IT SLIP THAT YOU'RE READY TO PAY THE BLACKMAILER'S FEE...

"BECAUSE ONE OF THEM IS SURE TO BE ON THE INSIDE AND WILL LET THE BLACKMAILER KNOW?

"YOU CATCH ON QUICK, KID.

"MEANWHILE, ALEX AND NATE WILL PREPARE OUR DECOY FOR THE RENDEZVOUS.

"WE HAVE A DECOY?

"NATE'S PARTNER, RONNIE. NO ONE INVOLVED HAS EVER SEEN HIM, SO THEY WON'T THINK TO PUT A TAIL ON HIM.

"AND WHAT'LL YOU BE DOING WHILE YOU LEAVE ME ALONE?"

"I'LL BE... FOLLOWING UP ON A HUNCH."

SO, IT'S THAT SORT OF PLACE. INTERESTING.

ROOMS AVAILABLE for rent by the week or day

DEERFIELD. WHAT'S HIS ROOM NUMBER?

WHOA THERE LIL' LADY, WHO WANTS TO KNOW?

YEAH, WHO THE HELL ARE YOU?

HIS TRUANT OFFICER.

HA HA HA! HEY FRED, DIDJA HEAR THAT ONE? "HIS TRUANT OFFICER"... WE GOT A REAL COMEDIENNE!

HE AIN'T HERE MUCH, LADY. YOU'D BE BETTER OFF TA CHECK HIS HQ OVER AT THE IMPERIAL PALACE HOTEL.

I JUST CAME FROM THERE. LOOK, TELL ME HIS ROOM NUMBER AND I PROMISE I'LL GIVE YOU ANY BOTTLES I FIND INSIDE.

NUMBER 16... BUT THERE AIN'T NOTHIN' IN THERE.

NOT EVEN A DROP. WE CHECKED. CHEAP BASTARD.

MUCH OBLIGED.

WELL, THIS'LL BE A QUICK SEARCH.

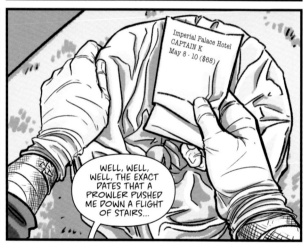

Imperial Palace Hotel
CAPTAIN K
May 8 - 10 ($68)

WELL, WELL, WELL, THE EXACT DATES THAT A PROWLER PUSHED ME DOWN A FLIGHT OF STAIRS...

HEY, HEY, WE DON'T ALLOW WHORES IN HERE! WHAT'RE YOU DOING IN THE CAPTAIN'S ROOM?

LEAVING.

Rooms Available
By the Week or Day

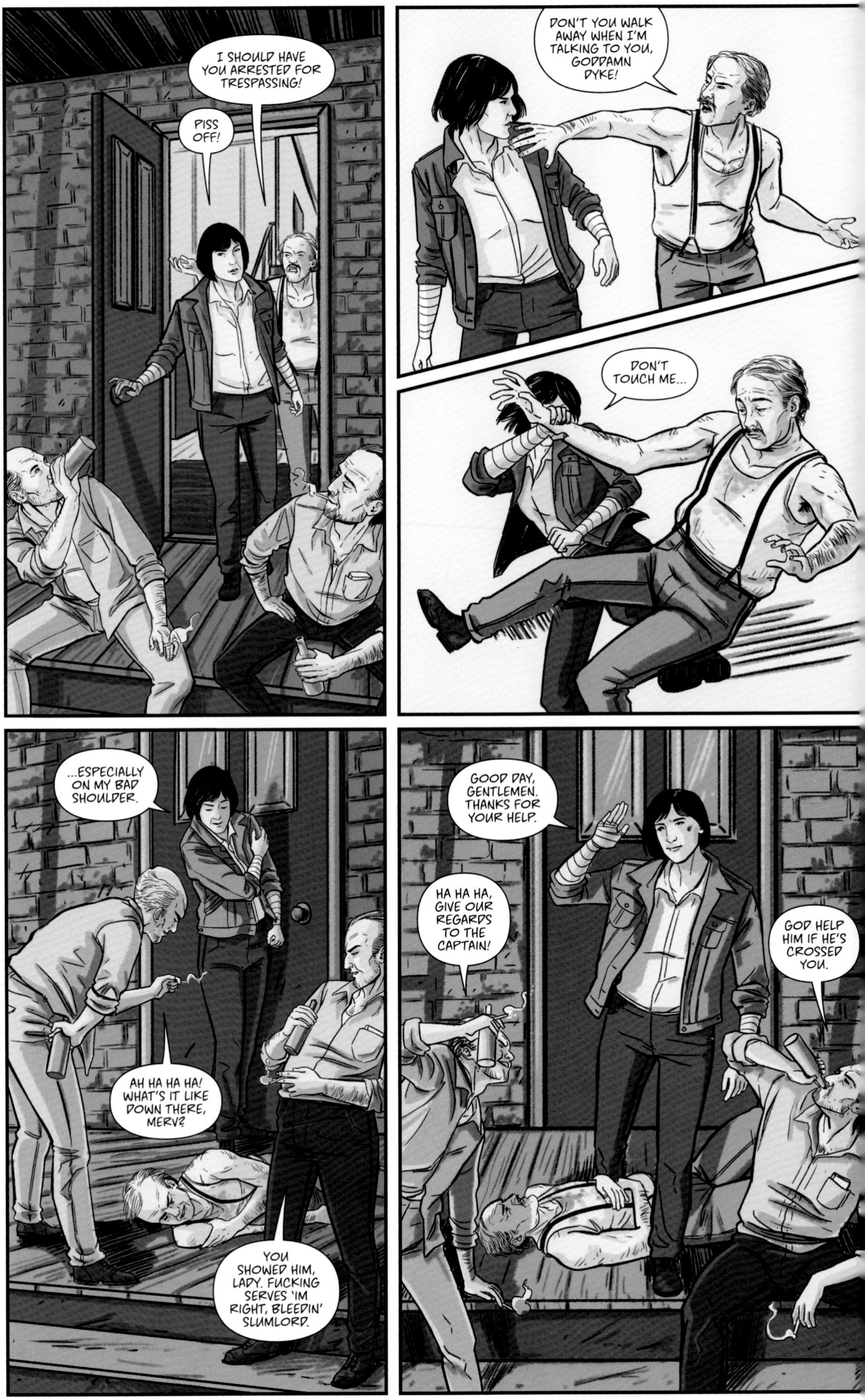
I SHOULD HAVE YOU ARRESTED FOR TRESPASSING!
PISS OFF!
DON'T YOU WALK AWAY WHEN I'M TALKING TO YOU, GODDAMN DYKE!
DON'T TOUCH ME...
...ESPECIALLY ON MY BAD SHOULDER.
AH HA HA HA! WHAT'S IT LIKE DOWN THERE, MERV?
YOU SHOWED HIM, LADY. FUCKING SERVES 'IM RIGHT, BLEEDIN' SLUMLORD.
GOOD DAY, GENTLEMEN. THANKS FOR YOUR HELP.
HA HA HA, GIVE OUR REGARDS TO THE CAPTAIN!
GOD HELP HIM IF HE'S CROSSED YOU.

HEY, NATE. I'M LOOKING FOR KARL DEERFIELD.

NOTHING ON KARL, BUT I DID GET MY HANDS ON THE CONTRACT SEDGWICK WANTS SONIA TO SIGN. AS YOU SUSPECTED, IT'S PRETTY SHADY.

THERE'S NO RECORDING DEAL WITH UNIVERSAL?

OH THERE'S A DEAL, BUT IT BENEFITS SEDGWICK ALMOST EXCLUSIVELY... UNIVERSAL DOESN'T CARE ABOUT SONIA, THEY JUST WANT TO KEEP THEIR RELATIONSHIP WITH SEDGWICK.

ONCE SONIA SIGNS WITH THEM, HE'LL OWN HER OUTRIGHT: EVERY MOVE, EVERY SONG. IT ISN'T ABOUT MONEY—

IT'S ABOUT CONTROLLING A BEAUTIFUL WOMAN... WELL, THAT EXPLAINS WHY HE'S SO AGAINST THIS MILLION. IF SHE REALIZES SHE DOESN'T NEED HIM, HE'S TOAST.

CALL BEN BONO, THIS SHOULD BE ENOUGH TO GET HIM TO HELP US OUT.

OKAY, I'LL HAVE BONO MEET US AT THE CAFÉ AROUND THE CORNER FROM HIS OFFICE.

WE GOTTA MAKE THIS FAST. THE SOONER I HAVE EYES ON UNCLE KARL, THE BETTER.

AN HOUR LATER.

I JUST DON'T UNDERSTAND WHY SEDGWICK WOULD DO THIS TO HER!

DO YOU KNOW ANY OTHER ENTRY-LEVEL CLIENT HE'D TAKE THIS MUCH INTEREST IN?

NO. BUT WHY WOULD HE BOTHER? IT CAN'T BE MONEY. HE SIGNED HER BEFORE SHE WON THE MILLION.

SO IF IT'S NOT MONEY, WHAT IS IT? IS HE ATTRACTED TO HER?

I MEAN, SHE'S BEAUTIFUL, SURE, BUT HE'S MARRIED! AND OLD ENOUGH TO BE HER FATHER!

AREN'T THEY ALL.

I WAS ALREADY SEEING SONIA WHEN HE MET HER. I TOOK HIM WITH ME TO THE CLUB ONE NIGHT TO HEAR HER SING. HE CONGRATULATED ME ON THE RELATIONSHIP!

SO HE CAN'T OWN HER, BUT YOU DO?

I DIDN'T SAY THAT. I LOVE HER. AND SHE LOVES ME.

HOW ROMANTIC.

SO HOW DID SEDGWICK ACT WHEN SONIA WON THE MONEY?

HE DIDN'T LIKE IT AT FIRST, BUT THEN AFTER A WHILE IT WAS BUSINESS AS USUAL.

HEH, I'LL BET.

IT TAKES QUITE A POWERFUL PERSONALITY TO HAVE ALL OF YOU OVERLOOK THE IMPLICATIONS OF THAT SUDDEN WEALTH. HOW FAR DO YOU THINK HE'D GO TO KEEP THAT POWER?

LOOK, HE'S CUNNING. I WOULDN'T WORK FOR HIM IF I WEREN'T. BUT HE'S TOO SAVVY TO HIRE A BLACKMAILER.

I THINK HE'S THE KIND OF MAN WHO WOULDN'T LET ANYTHING STOP HIM FROM GETTING WHAT HE WANTS. NOT YOU, AND CERTAINLY NOT ME... BY ANY MEANS NECESSARY.

HE'S TOO CLEAN FOR THAT. GET YOUR LICENSE REVOKED? SURE. BUT I CAN'T IMAGINE HIM GETTING TANGLED UP IN AN ATTEMPTED MURDER.

YEAH, IT SEEMS THERE'S A LOT YOU CAN'T IMAGINE.

YOU REALLY THINK HE DID IT?

THERE ARE MANY POSSIBILITIES. HAVE YOU SEEN ANYONE ELSE AROUND THE OFFICES? ANYONE UNUSUAL?

NOT THAT I CAN... OH, WELL, KARL DEERFIELD CAME BY TODAY. BUT SEDGWICK REFUSED TO MEET HIM.

WHAT TIME?

THIS MORNING. AROUND 11.

DID HE MENTION WHERE HE WAS HEADED?

HE WAS FURIOUS. HE SAID IF SEDGWICK WOULDN'T HELP HIM HE'D TALK TO WALTER. I STOPPED LISTENING AFTER THAT. WALTER AND SONIA HAVE BEEN DIVORCED FOR QUITE SOME TIME.

AND YOU DON'T LIKE BEING MADE TO FEEL LIKE A THIRD WHEEL. I'VE GOT TO RUN. DON'T BE SURPRISED IF YOU GET A CALL FROM THE POLICE ASKING WHAT WE CHATTED ABOUT.

YES, OF COURSE. I'LL TELL THE TRUTH, BUT WON'T OFFER ANY SPECULATION.

LOOK AT THAT, NATE. FREE ADVICE FROM A TOP-NOTCH LAWYER.

HEH. GOOD ADVICE TOO.

THE ANNEX.

RING!

RRRRING!

WALTER?! IT'S HELEN KEREMOS, I CAN SEE KARL'S CAR OUT FRONT. I KNOW YOU'RE BOTH IN THERE.

HELLO? I KNOW I'M NOT YOUR FAVOURITE PERSON, BUT THIS IS IMPORTANT...

FINE, WE'LL DO IT THE HARD WAY.

CLICK

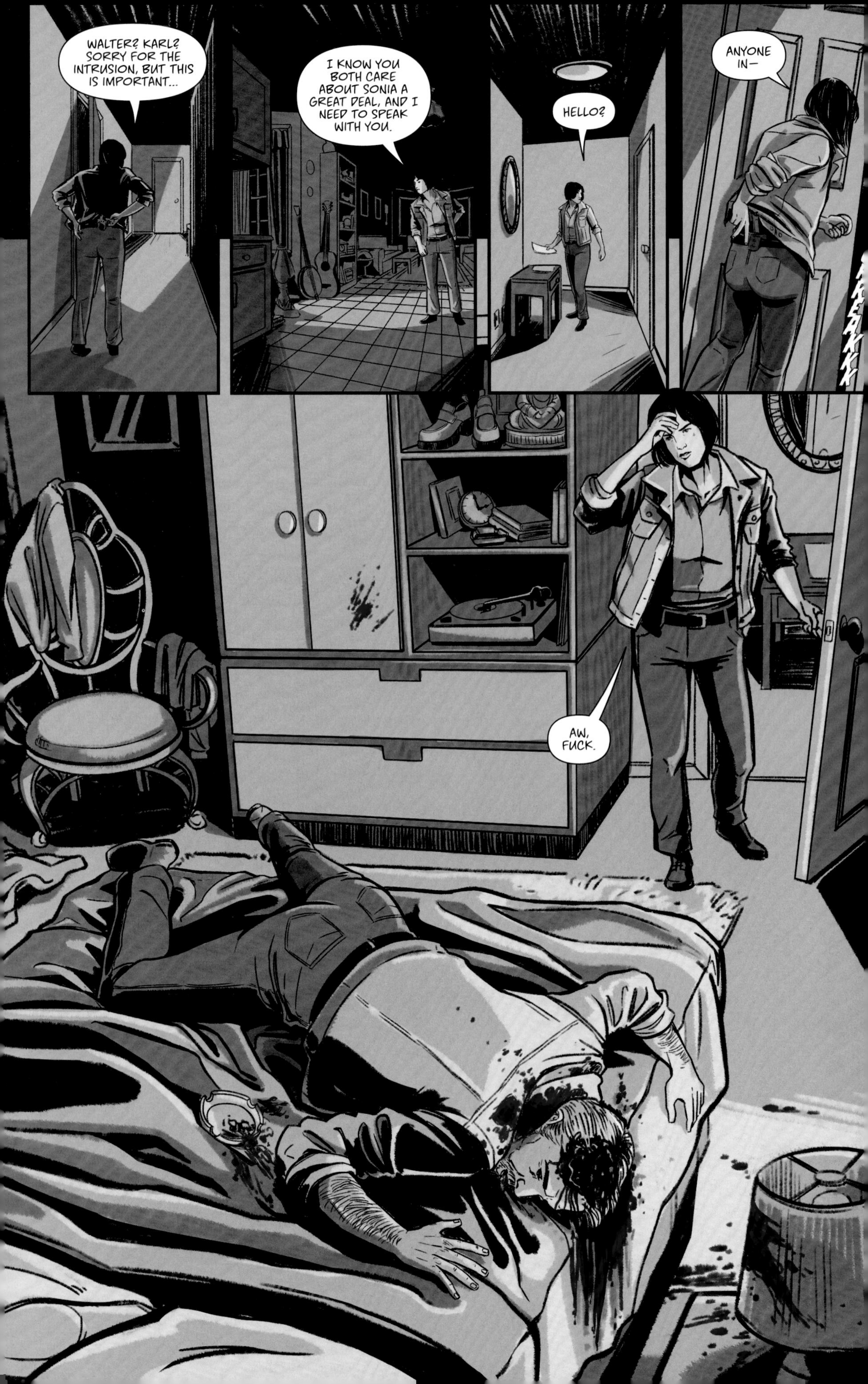

WALTER? KARL? SORRY FOR THE INTRUSION, BUT THIS IS IMPORTANT...
I KNOW YOU BOTH CARE ABOUT SONIA A GREAT DEAL, AND I NEED TO SPEAK WITH YOU.
HELLO?
ANYONE IN—
AW, FUCK.

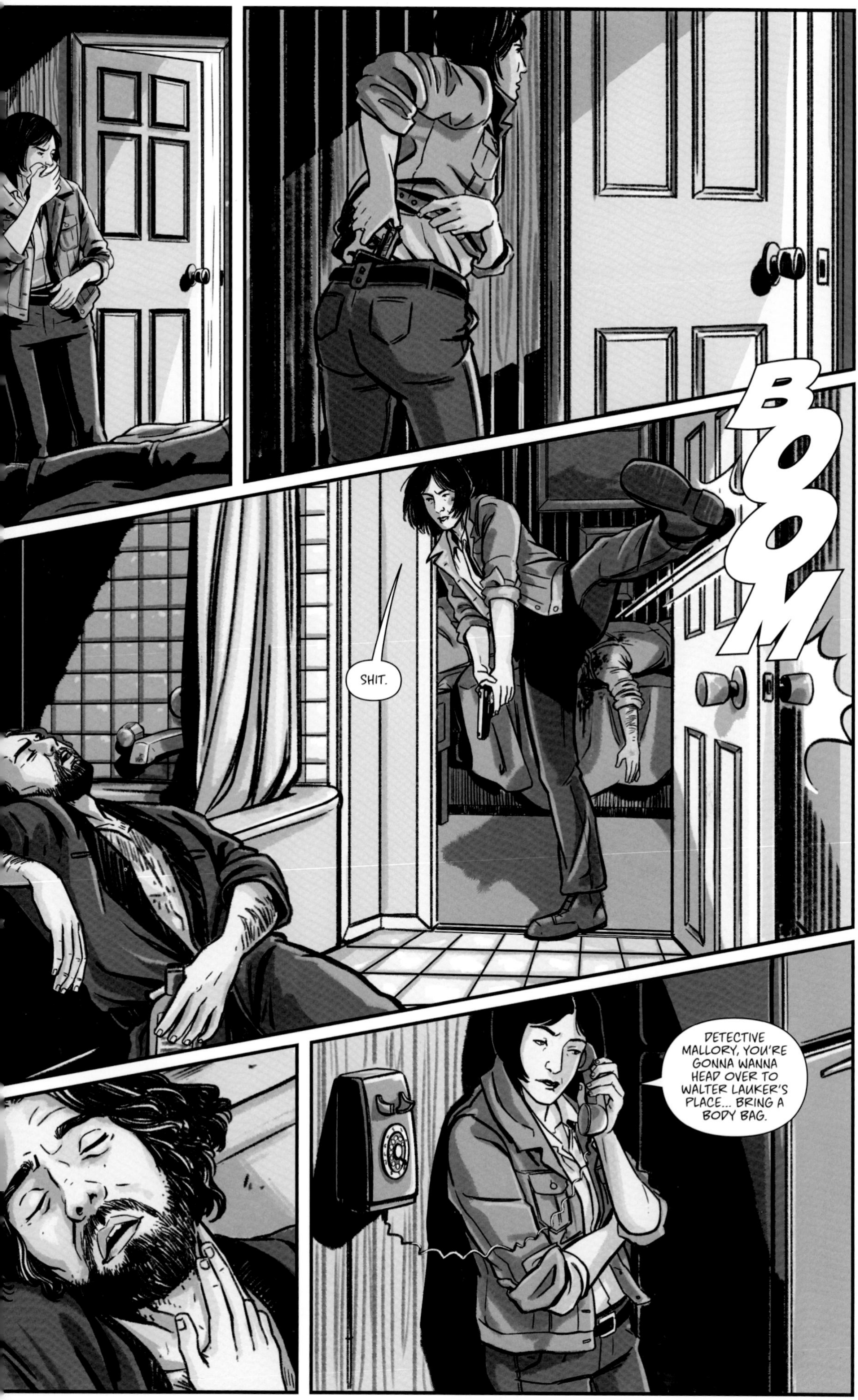
BOOM
SHIT.
DETECTIVE MALLORY, YOU'RE GONNA WANNA HEAD OVER TO WALTER LAUKER'S PLACE... BRING A BODY BAG.

SIX HOURS LATER.

I GUESS WE CAN WRAP IT UP FOR THE NIGHT. TOMORROW WE'LL START BACK-TRACKING, TYING LAUKER AND DEERFIELD TO THE BOMBINGS AND BLACKMAIL.

I CAN LET YOU LEAVE TORONTO IN A WEEK OR SO... YOU'LL HAVE TO BE BACK FOR THE TRIAL, OF COURSE.

INDEED.

WE'VE GOT A CUT-AND-DRY CASE HERE. I'D ADVISE YOU TO KEEP ANY UNFOUNDED SUSPICIONS TO YOURSELF.

YOU MEAN KEEP MY MOUTH SHUT AND DON'T TALK TO THE PRESS?

STOP BY THE POLICE STATION TOMORROW FOR A FORMAL DEPOSITION.

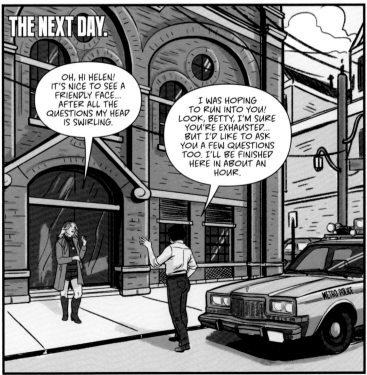

THE NEXT DAY.

OH, HI HELEN! IT'S NICE TO SEE A FRIENDLY FACE... AFTER ALL THE QUESTIONS MY HEAD IS SWIRLING.

I WAS HOPING TO RUN INTO YOU! LOOK, BETTY, I'M SURE YOU'RE EXHAUSTED... BUT I'D LIKE TO ASK YOU A FEW QUESTIONS TOO. I'LL BE FINISHED HERE IN ABOUT AN HOUR.

I'LL MAKE IT QUICK. SEE YOU BACK AT THE RITZ TEA ROOM AROUND 1?

I GUESS SO.

THAT WAS FAST. I FEEL LIKE *I* WAS THERE HALF THE DAY.

THEY DIDN'T WANT TO HEAR WHAT I HAD TO SAY.

WHAT'S THE STORY SO FAR?

THEY FOUND DYNAMITE IN KARL DEERFIELD'S ROOM FROM THE EXPLOSION, AND WALTER ISN'T TALKING.

HMMM.

I JUST CAN'T BELIEVE WALTER WOULD DO THIS.

OH COME ON, WALTER'S BEEN YOUR FAVOURITE SUSPECT FROM THE BEGINNING. EVERY ONE OF YOU MADE HIM FOR THE BLACKMAILER.

YEAH, BUT... MURDER?

IT IS AWFULLY CONVENIENT FOR THE PRIME SUSPECT TO BE CAUGHT RED-HANDED AT THE SCENE OF THE MURDER.

ISN'T IT THOUGH?

YOU'RE SKEPTICAL.

IT'S MY JOB TO BE.

DETECTIVE MALLORY ASKED ME IF IT WAS YOUR IDEA FOR SONIA TO OFFER TO PAY OFF THE BLACKMAILER. WAS IT?

IT DOESN'T MATTER NOW. THERE WON'T BE ANY MORE DEMANDS.

BECAUSE ANOTHER DEMAND WOULD MEAN IT COULDN'T HAVE BEEN WALTER AND KARL?

EXACTLY. OR AT LEAST IT'D MEAN THEY DIDN'T WORK ON THEIR OWN. AS LONG AS THE BLACKMAILER DOESN'T MAKE ANY MORE MOVES, THE CASE IS ALL TIED UP IN A PRETTY BOW. TALK ABOUT GETTING AWAY WITH MURDER.

YOU THINK IT WAS ONE OF US?

THE BLACKMAILER KNEW THINGS. WHERE SONIA WAS GOING, WHAT SHE WAS DOING... I THINK IT'S LIKELY SOMEONE SHE TRUSTS EVEN MORE THAN WALTER.

WELL, THAT COULD ONLY BE ME OR... LEW. YOU DON'T THINK—

NO ONE IS ACCUSING YOU OF ANYTHING, BETTY.

I SHOULD REALLY GET GOING. THANKS FOR THE TEA.

ALEX, WILL YOU HEAD OVER TO THE HOTEL AND KEEP AN EYE ON SONIA?

I NEED TO HAVE A LITTLE CHAT WITH LEW DAVIES.

BUT FIRST, YOU NEED TO LOSE YOUR LITTLE FRIEND.

I LOVE IT WHEN YOU GET THE SMARTS.

TORONTO'S FINEST AREN'T THE MOST SUBTLE. I'LL GIVE YOU A LITTLE HEAD START.

OH MY GOODNESS, I AM SO, SO SORRY! LET ME HELP YOU CLEAN THIS UP!

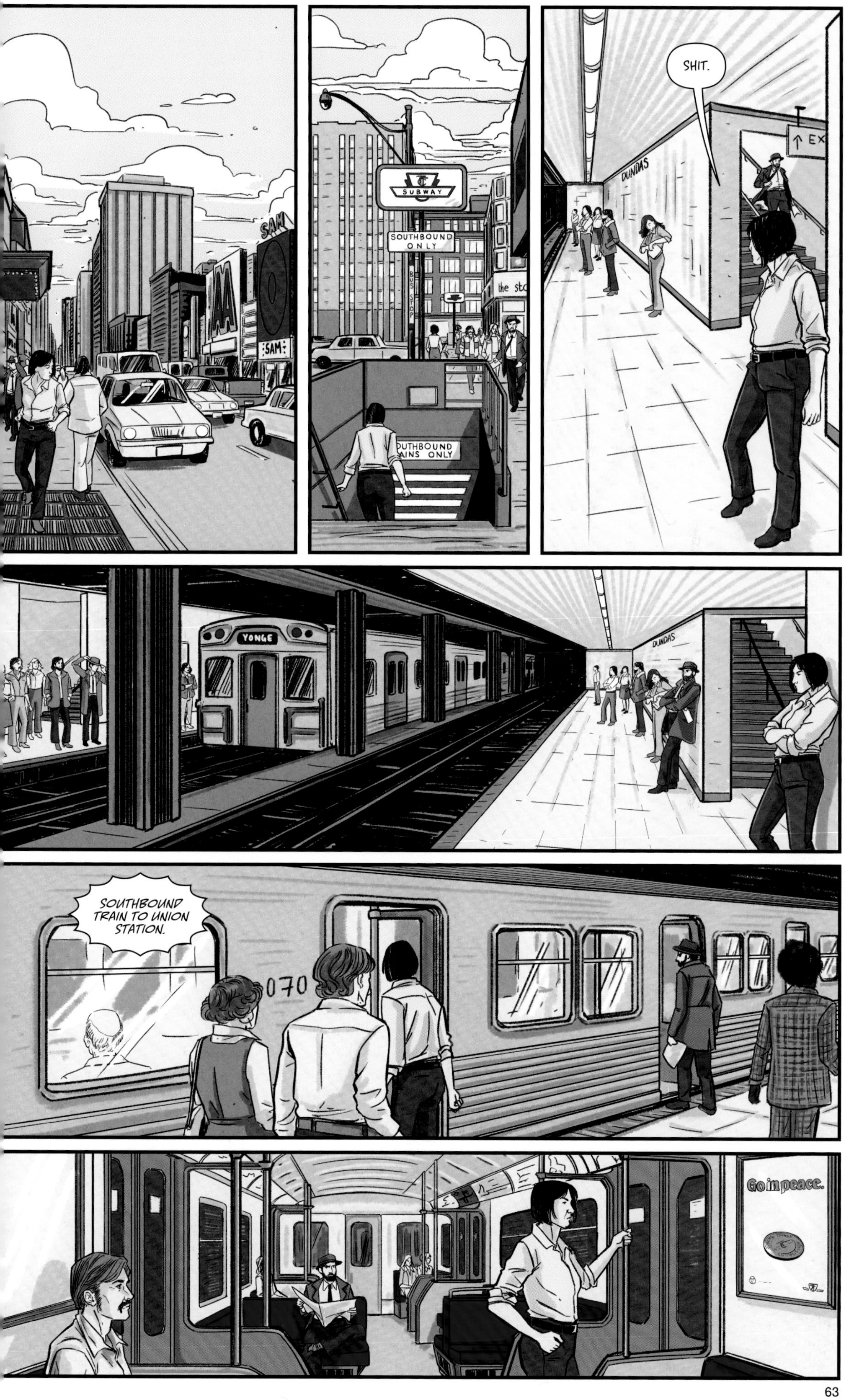
SAM
SAM
SUBWAY
SOUTHBOUND ONLY
BUS STOP
the sto
UTHBOUND
AINS ONLY
SHIT.
DUNDAS
EX
YONGE
DUNDAS
SOUTHBOUND TRAIN TO UNION STATION.
070
Go in peace.

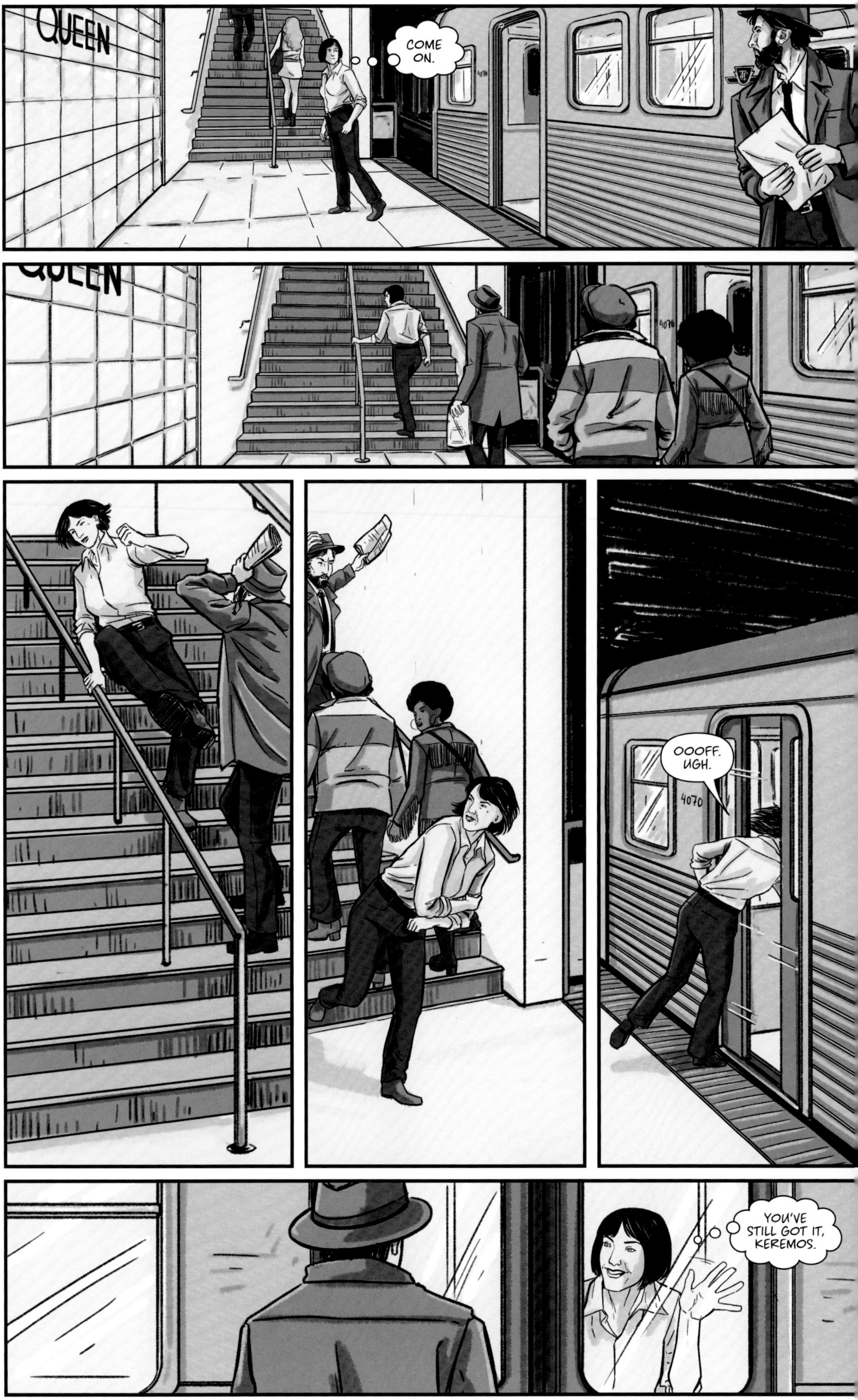
COME ON.
QUEEN
OOOFF. UGH.
YOU'VE STILL GOT IT, KEREMOS.

CABBAGETOWN.

WELL....THAT'S CERTAINLY A STATEMENT.

OOF.

CREAK

Clink

AND THE BLUE JAYS ARE UP BY FOUR RUNS IN THE BOTTOM OF THE SIXTH...

MIND IF I JOIN YOU?

WHAT THE—?!

WE BOTH KNOW THE JAYS WILL CHOKE BEFORE THE GAME'S OVER.

WHAT ARE YOU DOING IN MY HOUSE?!

I CAME IN THROUGH THE BACK SO I WOULDN'T DISTURB METRO'S FINEST. NOTICE ANYONE?

CLICK

WHY WOULD I? THE POLICE HAVE NO REASON TO BE WATCHING ME.

WALT KILLING KARL AND THEN PASSING OUT WITH THE MURDER WEAPON RIGHT THERE AT THE SCENE OF THE CRIME... IT'S VERY CONVENIENT.

THEY HAD TO BE WORKING TOGETHER! THEY FOUND THE BOMBING EVIDENCE IN KARL'S APARTMENT!

THEY SURE DID. THE PROBLEM IS, I WAS IN KARL'S APARTMENT BEFORE HE WAS KILLED AND I DIDN'T SEE ANY DYNAMITE. PLUS, EVEN IF KARL DID IT, THAT DOESN'T PROVE WALT WAS HIS ACCOMPLICE.

LET'S THINK ABOUT THE POSSIBILITIES: SEDGWICK DOESN'T SEEM LIKE THE KIND OF MAN WHO'D WANT KARL ON HIS HANDS. I DOUBT HE'D GO INTO THE BLACKMAIL BUSINESS WITH HIM.

BEN BONO WANTS TO MARRY SONIA. BLEEDING HER DRY DOESN'T MAKE MUCH SENSE. SO WHO DOES THAT LEAVE?

BESIDES WALT? BETTY... AND ME. WHAT ARE YOU DRIVING AT HERE?

IF YOU HAVE SOME SORT OF EVIDENCE SPILL IT OR I'LL CALL THE POLICE AND GET YOU OUT OF THE HOUSE MYSELF.

GO AHEAD. I'M SURE SONIA WILL LOVE TO KNOW YOU WERE TOO NERVOUS TO CHAT WITH ME. NOT THAT I SEE HER TRUSTING ANYONE IN HER INNER CIRCLE AFTER THIS.

RING! RING!

SHE'S BEEN BETRAYED BY WALT, THAT'S GONNA STING. BUT I'VE ALWAYS BEEN THERE FOR HER. THEY'VE GOT HIM NOW AND SOON THINGS WILL GO BACK TO NORMAL.

HELLO? OH, HI BETTY, I....

WHAT?

SHE'S HERE ACTUALLY.

IT'S BETTY.

HELEN! HELEN, LISTEN. I WAS JUST TELLING LEW. WALT IS OUT OF CUSTODY. HE'S COMING HERE—

WHERE IS "HERE?"

HELEN! THEY LET WALT GO! HE WAS RELEASED THIS AFTERNOON AND NOW HE SAYS HE SUDDENLY REMEMBERS SOMETHING.

DETECTIVE MALLORY IS ON HIS WAY OVER HERE AND I THINK YOU SHOULD BE TOO... HE ALSO REQUESTED LEW. THAT'S WHY WE CALLED.

WE'RE ON OUR WAY.

WHAT HAPPENED?

IN LIGHT OF NEW EVIDENCE—

ANOTHER EXTORTION ATTEMPT WAS MADE AFTER WALT WAS ARRESTED, BUT I HADN'T BEEN HOME TO CHECK MY ANSWERING SERVICE, SO WE ONLY JUST FOUND OUT.

ALEX?

I WAS WITH HER WHEN SHE GOT THE MESSAGE. I CALLED THE SERVICE AND MADE SURE THEY GAVE ME EVERY DETAIL FROM THE ORIGINAL MESSAGE SLIP. A MAN'S VOICE SAID "TWO HUNDRED THOUSAND IS THE NUMBER. GET IT TOGETHER. PLACE AND TIME TO FOLLOW."

YOU SAID THERE WOULDN'T BE ANY MORE EXTORTION DEMANDS!

APPARENTLY OUR BLACKMAILER DIDN'T GET THE MEMO.

AND HELEN, I TOLD DETECTIVE MALLORY ABOUT UNCLE KARL. I WANTED HIM TO KNOW WHY I'D TESTIFY THAT WALT WOULD NEVER, UNDER ANY CIRCUMSTANCES, LET KARL HANDLE MY MONEY.

AND NOW I'M OUT OF THE DUNGEON! I'M FREE TO ONCE AGAIN BE AT THE FEET OF MY GORGEOUS SONIA.

YES, I AM GLAD YOU'RE FREE, BUT PLEASE JUST TELL US WHAT YOU KNOW. THE POLICE ARE HELPLESS WITHOUT YOUR INFORMATION.

HELPLESS?! NOW I—

VERY WELL. I WAS IN MY HUMBLE ABODE, HAVING A LATE SNACK WITH HEROD.

THAT'S HIS CAT.

"AND WHO SHOULD SUDDENLY PRESENT HIMSELF, BUT DEAR OLD UNCLE KARL, COMPLAINING THAT HE WAS BEING HARASSED BY HELEN AND DEMANDING I HELP HIM KEEP SONIA SAFE.

I DIDN'T BUY HIS 'ALTRUISM' FOR A MOMENT AND REMINDED HIM THAT SONIA IS A GROWN WOMAN. KARL SEEMED PERFECTLY AWARE SONIA LOATHES HIM... HE JUST DIDN'T CARE.

HE WAS PROUD OF HIS MANEUVERS AROUND SONIA. OF COURSE, HE SAID IT WAS ALL 'FOR HER OWN GOOD': THE CALLS, THE VANDALISM, EVEN THE BOMB... THAT WAS AIMED AT HELEN, OF COURSE.

NOW I MAY NOT BE THE BRIGHTEST MAN, BUT I KNEW KARL COULDN'T HAVE PULLED ALL THIS OFF ALONE. AND JUST AS I WAS ASKING ABOUT THAT... WELL, WHO KNOCKED ON MY DOOR BUT OUR OWN DEAR LEW DAVIES?

SEE, OUR FRIEND HERE CAME LOOKING FOR KARL, AND AFTER HE REALIZED KARL HAD ALREADY SPILLED THE BEANS TO ME... WELL, HE GOT VERY GENEROUS.

WHILE I WAS, UH, BENEFITTING FROM HIS GENEROSITY... LEW DECIDED TO TELL ME HIS SIDE OF THE STORY. HE WAS ONLY HELPING UNCLE KARL REACH HIS PROPER PLACE AT SONIA'S SIDE...

SO THEN I HAD TO EXPLAIN TO THE POOR FOOL WHY UNCLE KARL WAS THE ABSOLUTE LAST PERSON IN THE WORLD THAT OUR DEAR SONIA WOULD ALLOW NEAR HER IN ANY CIRCUMSTANCE."

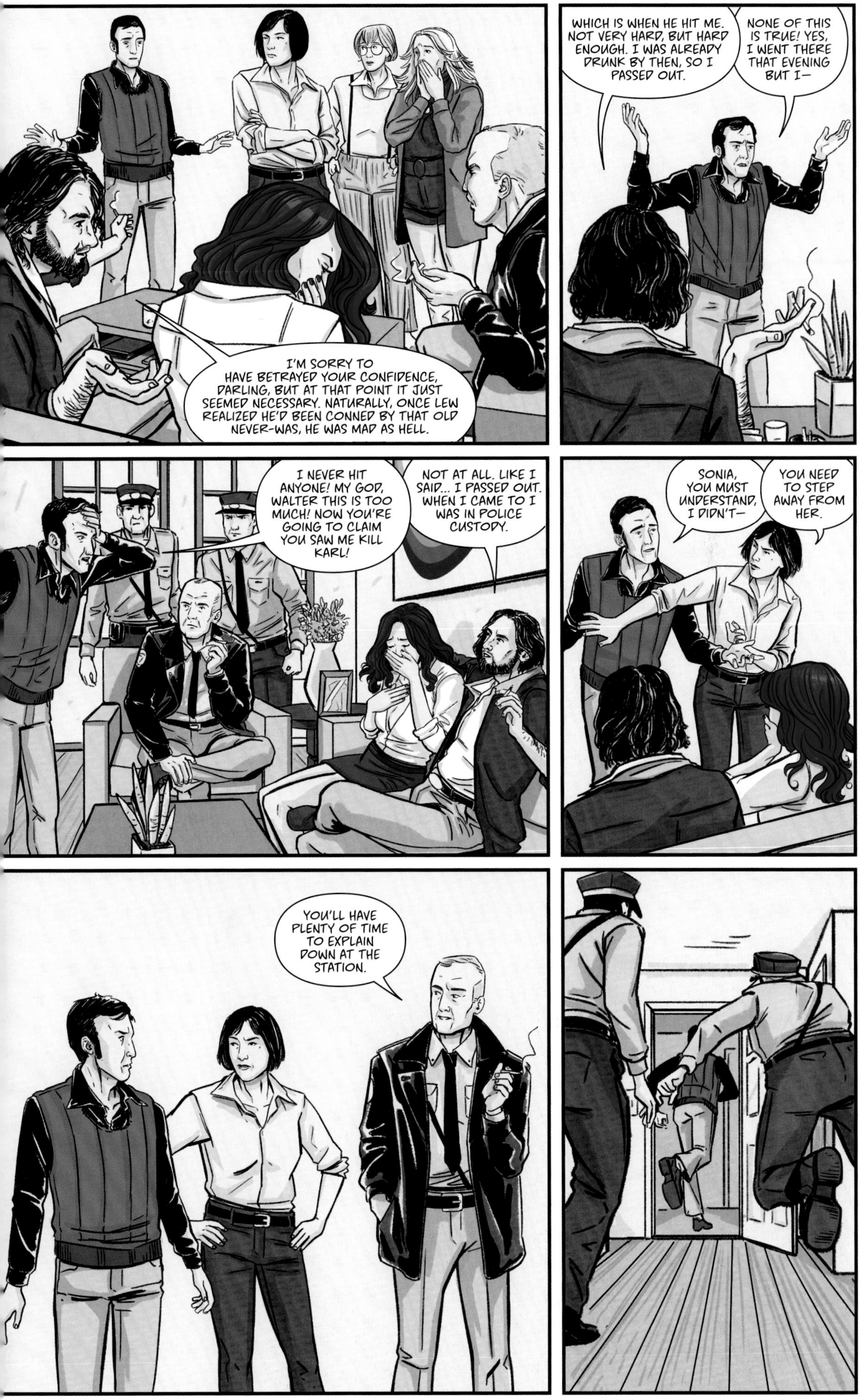
I'M SORRY TO HAVE BETRAYED YOUR CONFIDENCE, DARLING, BUT AT THAT POINT IT JUST SEEMED NECESSARY. NATURALLY, ONCE LEW REALIZED HE'D BEEN CONNED BY THAT OLD NEVER-WAS, HE WAS MAD AS HELL.
WHICH IS WHEN HE HIT ME. NOT VERY HARD, BUT HARD ENOUGH. I WAS ALREADY DRUNK BY THEN, SO I PASSED OUT.
NONE OF THIS IS TRUE! YES, I WENT THERE THAT EVENING BUT I—
I NEVER HIT ANYONE! MY GOD, WALTER THIS IS TOO MUCH! NOW YOU'RE GOING TO CLAIM YOU SAW ME KILL KARL!
NOT AT ALL. LIKE I SAID... I PASSED OUT. WHEN I CAME TO I WAS IN POLICE CUSTODY.
SONIA, YOU MUST UNDERSTAND, I DIDN'T—
YOU NEED TO STEP AWAY FROM HER.
YOU'LL HAVE PLENTY OF TIME TO EXPLAIN DOWN AT THE STATION.

WE PUT AN APB OUT ON HIS PLATE.

BUT THEY LOST HIM.

I BROUGHT LEW IN. IT WAS UP TO *YOU* TO HOLD HIM.

HELP ME GET EVERYONE OUT OF HERE. SONIA NEEDS REST.

HOW YA DOING?

I JUST FOUND OUT ONE OF THE PEOPLE CLOSEST TO ME IS A LIAR WHO ENDANGERED MY LIFE... SO, YOU KNOW, NOT MUCH HAS CHANGED.

WE MAY NEED TO RETHINK YOUR VETTING PROCESS IN THE FUTURE.

HA! I'M RETHINKING A LOT OF THINGS... FRIENDS, CAREER, MY RELATIONSHIP WITH BEN... I'M JUST...

...QUESTIONING EVERYTHING.

GET SOME REST. YOU'VE BEEN THROUGH HELL TODAY. HOPEFULLY THE POLICE WILL HAVE FOUND LEW FOR QUESTIONING BY TOMORROW.

BETTY'S GONE HOME, FINALLY. I ASKED HER WHERE SHE THOUGHT LEW WOULD GO, BUT SHE SAID THERE ARE ONLY TWO PEOPLE HE WOULD TRUST AT A TIME LIKE THIS: SONIA AND...

...HER.

OKAY, WE'LL MAKE SURE SHE MEETS US BACK HERE FIRST THING TOMORROW. I'M GONNA GET A LITTLE SHUT EYE. YOU SHOULD TOO.

HEY, KEREMOS... MAKE SURE YOUR FEELINGS FOR YOUR CLIENT DON'T START CLOUDING YOUR JUDGMENT.

I'LL TAKE THAT UNDER ADVISEMENT.

RING! RING! RING!

RING! RING!

CALM DOWN. BETTY. OKAY, OKAY, I'LL BE THERE.

BETTY'S BEEN KIDNAPPED. SHE SAID "TAKE $200,000 AND GO TO THE RITZ."

CAN YOU GET THE CASH HERE QUICKLY... AND DISCREETLY?

GIVE ME AN HOUR.

OKAY, RONNIE. JUST STRIDE OUT WITH CONFIDENCE AND NO ONE SHOULD PAY YOU ANY MIND. MALLORY AND HIS MEN HAVEN'T SEEN YOU BEFORE, SO HOPEFULLY THEY'LL IGNORE THE BAG. MEET ME AT THE CORNER OF YONGE AND CHARLES.

MAYBE RIGHT IN THE CHARLES STREET PROMENADE? I COULD WANDER AROUND LIKE A TOURIST?

JUST BE A CAUTIOUS TOURIST. I DON'T WANT YOU TO END UP WITH A GUN TO YOUR HEAD.

I'LL TAKE GOOD CARE OF HIM, NATE.

IMPERIAL PALACE
Hotel Guest Parking Only

THE RITZ, PLEASE, BUT DROP ME OFF ON THE CORNER OF CHARLES STREET AT BAY, NOT YONGE... I'M TRYING TO SURPRISE SOMEONE.

A LITTLE BIRTHDAY CELEBRATION AT THE RITZ, EH?

SOMETHING LIKE THAT.

BAY

KEEP WALKING, I'LL STEER. THIS IS A GUN.

I DIDN'T THINK IT WAS A BOUQUET OF FLOWERS.

WHERE'S THE MONEY?

NEAR.

WHY DON'T YOU HAVE IT WITH YOU?

THE SAME REASON I DIDN'T LET SONIA MAKE THE DELIVERY. I'M NOT RECKLESS.

74

CLOMP! CLOMP! CLOMP!

OH, CLEVER.

GET INSIDE.

OUT OF ORDER

I'M GONNA UNTIE BETTY, THIS MUST BE UNCOMFORTABLE FOR HER. DON'T TRY ANYTHING.

I'M NOT GOING ANYWHERE.

I NEED YOU TO GET ME TO SONIA SO I CAN EXPLAIN.

EXPLAIN WHAT? YOU SPLIT THE SECOND LAUKER ACCUSED YOU OF KILLING DEERFIELD. NOT EXACTLY A GOOD LOOK. THE ONLY EXPLAINING YOU CAN DO IS TO THE POLICE.

I DON'T TRUST THE COPS. SONIA KNOWS ME. SHE'LL BELIEVE ME. THAT'S WHAT MATTERS NOW. I'VE NOTHING ELSE TO LOSE. I DIDN'T MURDER KARL.

BUT THAT'S NOT ALL, IS IT? THERE ARE THE CALLS, THE EXTORTION, THE BOMB... ARE YOU INNOCENT IN ALL THAT AS WELL?

I HAD NOTHING TO DO WITH THE BOMB! KARL DIDN'T TELL ME ABOUT THE BOMB UNTIL AFTER! I... I DON'T NEED TO DISCUSS THIS WITH YOU.

OH COME ON, LEW. IT'S OVER. WE HAVE TO TELL HELEN EVERYTHING. IT'S OUR ONLY CHANCE.

YOU STUPID BITCH! I TRIED TO KEEP YOU OUT OF THIS!

HEY NOW—

LEW, IT WON'T WORK. JUST TELL HELEN THE TRUTH AND THEN SHE'LL HELP US. I KNOW SHE WILL.

YOU ALREADY KNOW SEDGWICK AND BONO MUSCLED IN ON US. AT FIRST WE WERE HAPPY FOR SONIA—SHE WAS GETTING MORE EXPOSURE. IT WAS HARD... BUT EVERYTHING WE DID, WE DID OUT OF LOVE FOR SONIA.

I'M SURE THAT'S WHAT YOU TELL YOURSELVES.

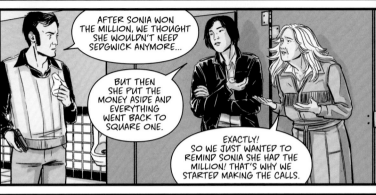

AFTER SONIA WON THE MILLION, WE THOUGHT SHE WOULDN'T NEED SEDGWICK ANYMORE...

BUT THEN SHE PUT THE MONEY ASIDE AND EVERYTHING WENT BACK TO SQUARE ONE.

EXACTLY! SO WE JUST WANTED TO REMIND SONIA SHE HAD THE MILLION! THAT'S WHY WE STARTED MAKING THE CALLS.

YOU WEREN'T WORRIED THAT WOULD BACKFIRE? THAT SHE'D GIVE SEDGWICK THE MONEY TO HANDLE?

OH, WE MADE IT CLEAR IN THE CALLS THAT WOULDN'T GET HER OFF THE HOOK.

ANYWAY, WE WENT IN AS A JOKE ALMOST. WE DIDN'T REALLY THINK ABOUT IT! AND AFTER SONIA STARTED GETTING STRESSED, WE REALIZED IT WASN'T WORKING. WE WERE GONNA BACK OFF!

SO WHY DIDN'T YOU?

KARL. I DON'T KNOW HOW HE FOUND OUT WHAT WE WERE DOING, BUT HE CORNERED US AND MADE A PROPOSITION.

HE'D KEEP OUR SECRET IF WE PERSUADED SONIA TO LET HIM BE HER FINANCIAL ADVISER.

AND YOU FELL FOR THAT?

I DIDN'T KNOW ABOUT THEIR PAST! I WOULD HAVE NEVER AGREED.

AND THEN IT ALL GOT OUT OF HAND. HE TOOK OVER AND DID THINGS WE DIDN'T KNOW ABOUT. LIKE THE BOMB... HE TOOK IT TOO FAR.

IT WAS ALL TOO FAR. SOME FRIENDS YOU ARE.

AND THE NIGHT KARL DIED?

I WAS THERE, BUT WHEN I LEFT, EVERYONE WAS CONSCIOUS AND ALIVE. I'LL TALK TO THE POLICE BUT I JUST WANT A CHANCE TO SEE SONIA FIRST. SHE DESERVES THAT MUCH.

WILL YOU HELP US SPEAK TO HER, HELEN?

I'LL SPEAK TO SONIA AND THEN SHE CAN DECIDE WHAT SHE DESERVES. DO YOU HAVE A CAR?

SO YOU DIDN'T PLANT THE EXPLOSIVES AT KARL'S THE NIGHT OF THE MURDER?

NO, BUT I KNOW HE WAS BEHIND THE BOMBING. WALT'S RIGHT THAT HE BRAGGED ABOUT IT.

IMPERIAL PALACE
Hotel Guest Parking Only

... ARE WALTER AND SONIA STILL MARRIED?

LEGALLY, YEAH SURE, BUT THEY'VE BEEN SEPARATED FOR WELL OVER A YEAR NOW.

RIGHT. SO WHO INHERITS IN THE EVENT OF HER DEATH?

OH...

"OH" IS RIGHT.

HANG TIGHT. I MEAN IT.

I BELIEVE YOU DIDN'T MURDER KARL. AND I'LL HELP YOU PROVE IT. BUT I SWEAR IF YOU MOVE SO MUCH AS A WHEEL OUTSIDE OF THIS PARKING SPACE BEFORE I GET BACK...

YOU'VE GOT OUR WORD, HELEN.

A LOT OF GOOD THAT DID SONIA.

HELEN... THANKS.

YEAH, YEAH, JUST DON'T MAKE ME A SUCKER, TOO.

SHIT.

RONNIE?! RONNIE!

UNNNN...

WHAT HAPPENED? WHERE'S THE BACKPACK? WHO FOLLOWED YOU HERE?

SHIT.

LOBBY

WE'VE GOT A SITUATION. SEE ANYONE?

NOTHING UNUSUAL. LOOK, THIS IS NOT GONNA BE GOOD FOR THE HOTEL—

BLAST THE HOTEL, CHESTER. GO UP TO SONIA'S ROOM AND SEN[D] ALEX AND NATE DOWN. STAY WITH SONIA TIL' WE GET THERE.

ARE YOU OKAY, HONEY?

JUST A HEADACHE. IT'LL BE FINE. I GOT CLOCKED FROM BEHIND, I DON'T KNOW WHO HIT ME, BUT WHOEVER IT WAS KNEW I HAD A BACKPACK FULL OF CASH.

GET HIM TO A HOSPITAL AND HAVE HIM CHECKED FOR A CONCUSSION. AND RONNIE, IF YOU REMEMBER ANYTHING YOU THINK IS IMPORTANT CALL ME, OKAY?

YOU GOT IT.

I KNOW THAT LOOK... YOU'RE TRYING TO WORK SOMETHING OUT.

I WAS WITH BONNIE AND LEW... SO WHO ELSE KNEW ABOUT THE MONEY... AND HOW DID THEY KNOW RONNIE HAD A BACKPACK... OR THAT HE'D BE HEADING BACK TO THE HOTEL?

CHESTER!

SHE'S GONE. CALL DETECTIVE MALLORY AND GET AN AMBULANCE FOR CHESTER.

ON IT.

BE CAREFUL!

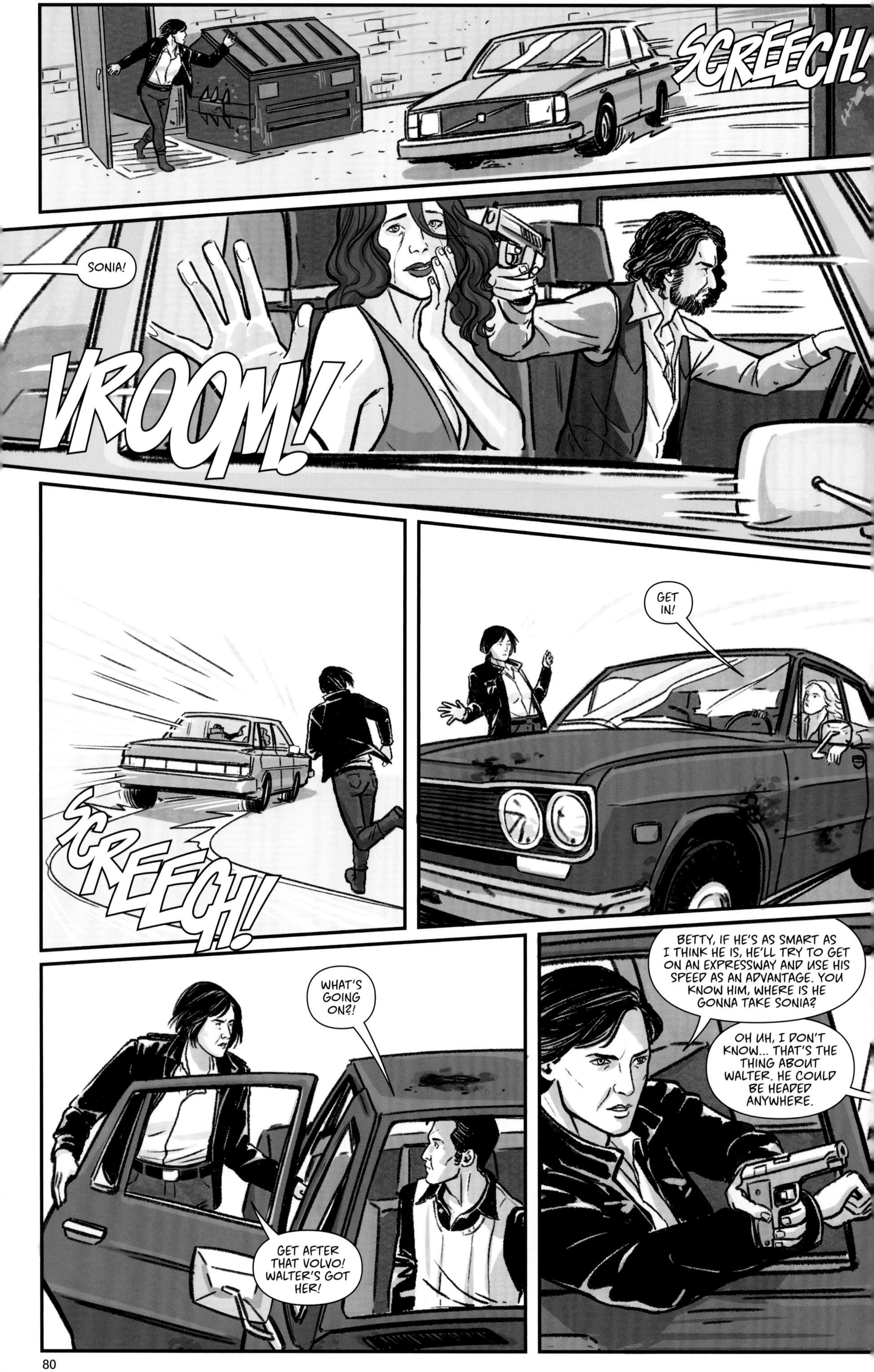
SCREECH!
SONIA!
VROOM!
SCREECH!
GET IN!
WHAT'S GOING ON?!
GET AFTER THAT VOLVO! WALTER'S GOT HER!
BETTY, IF HE'S AS SMART AS I THINK HE IS, HE'LL TRY TO GET ON AN EXPRESSWAY AND USE HIS SPEED AS AN ADVANTAGE. YOU KNOW HIM, WHERE IS HE GONNA TAKE SONIA?
OH UH, I DON'T KNOW... THAT'S THE THING ABOUT WALTER. HE COULD BE HEADED ANYWHERE.

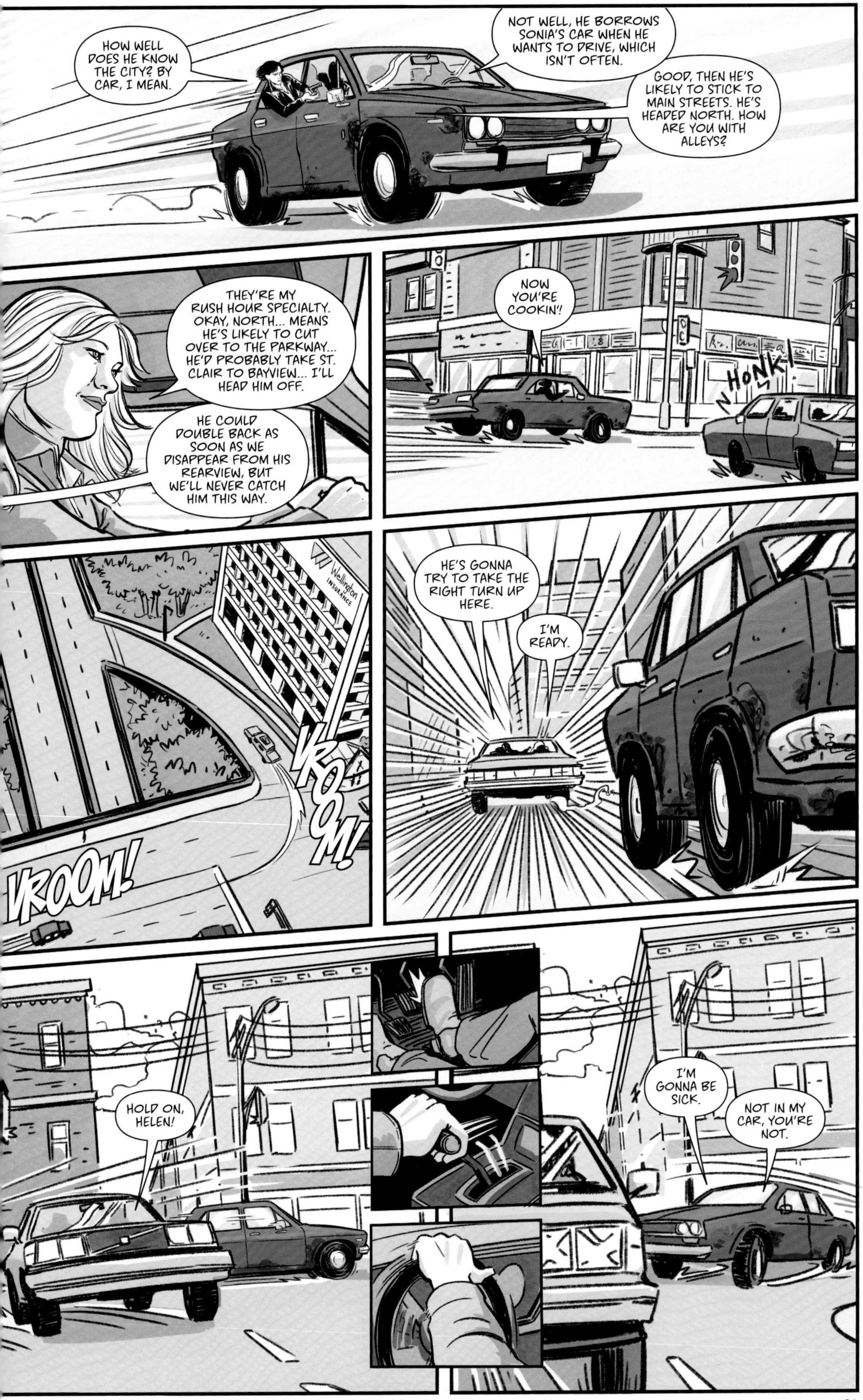
HOW WELL DOES HE KNOW THE CITY? BY CAR, I MEAN.
NOT WELL, HE BORROWS SONIA'S CAR WHEN HE WANTS TO DRIVE, WHICH ISN'T OFTEN.
GOOD, THEN HE'S LIKELY TO STICK TO MAIN STREETS. HE'S HEADED NORTH. HOW ARE YOU WITH ALLEYS?
THEY'RE MY RUSH HOUR SPECIALTY. OKAY, NORTH... MEANS HE'S LIKELY TO CUT OVER TO THE PARKWAY... HE'D PROBABLY TAKE ST. CLAIR TO BAYVIEW... I'LL HEAD HIM OFF.
HE COULD DOUBLE BACK AS SOON AS WE DISAPPEAR FROM HIS REARVIEW, BUT WE'LL NEVER CATCH HIM THIS WAY.
NOW YOU'RE COOKIN'!
HONK!
Wellington INSURANCE
VROOM!
VROOM!
HE'S GONNA TRY TO TAKE THE RIGHT TURN UP HERE.
I'M READY.
HOLD ON, HELEN!
I'M GONNA BE SICK.
NOT IN MY CAR, YOU'RE NOT.

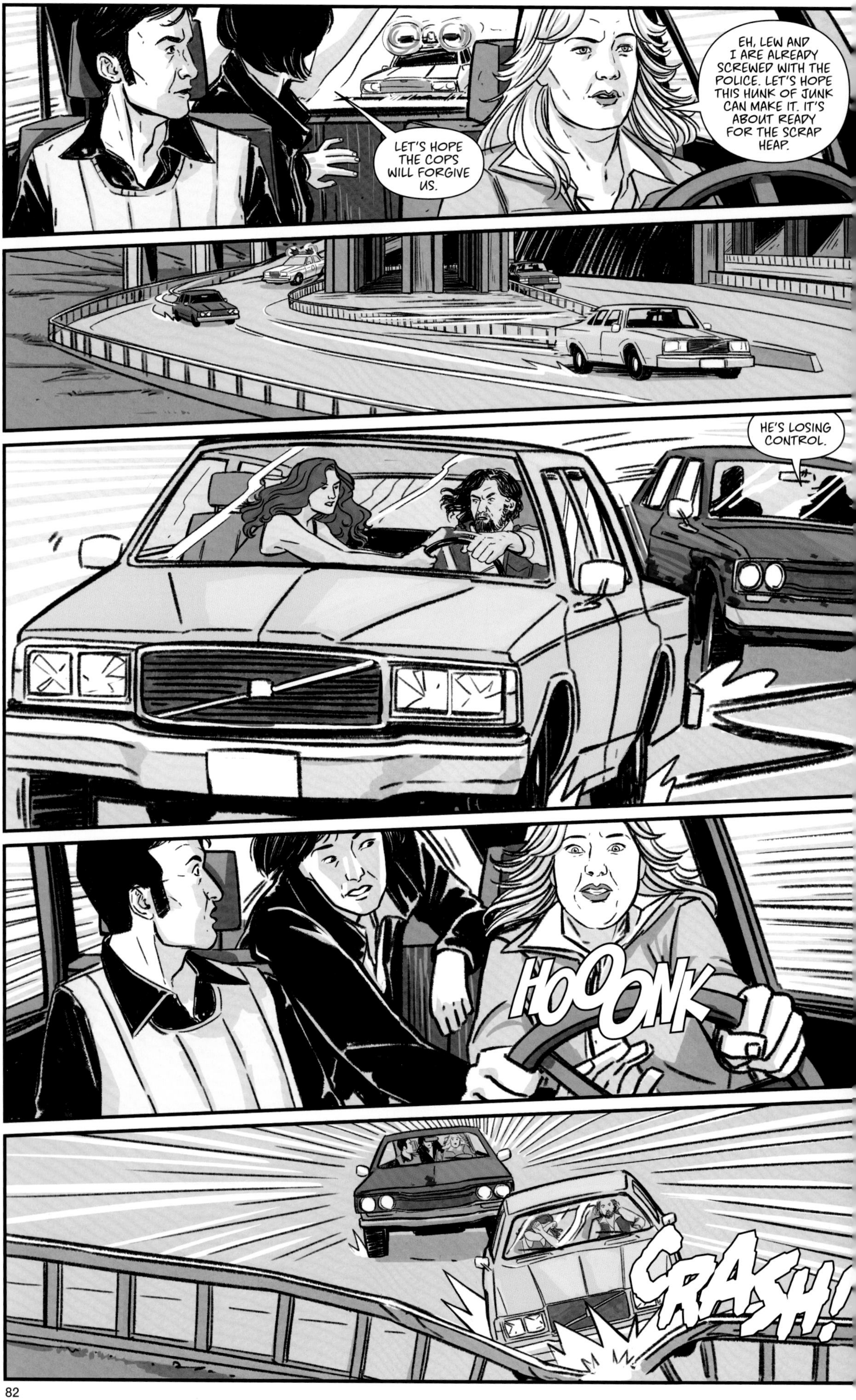
LET'S HOPE THE COPS WILL FORGIVE US.
EH, LEW AND I ARE ALREADY SCREWED WITH THE POLICE. LET'S HOPE THIS HUNK OF JUNK CAN MAKE IT. IT'S ABOUT READY FOR THE SCRAP HEAP.
HE'S LOSING CONTROL.
HOOONK
CRASH!

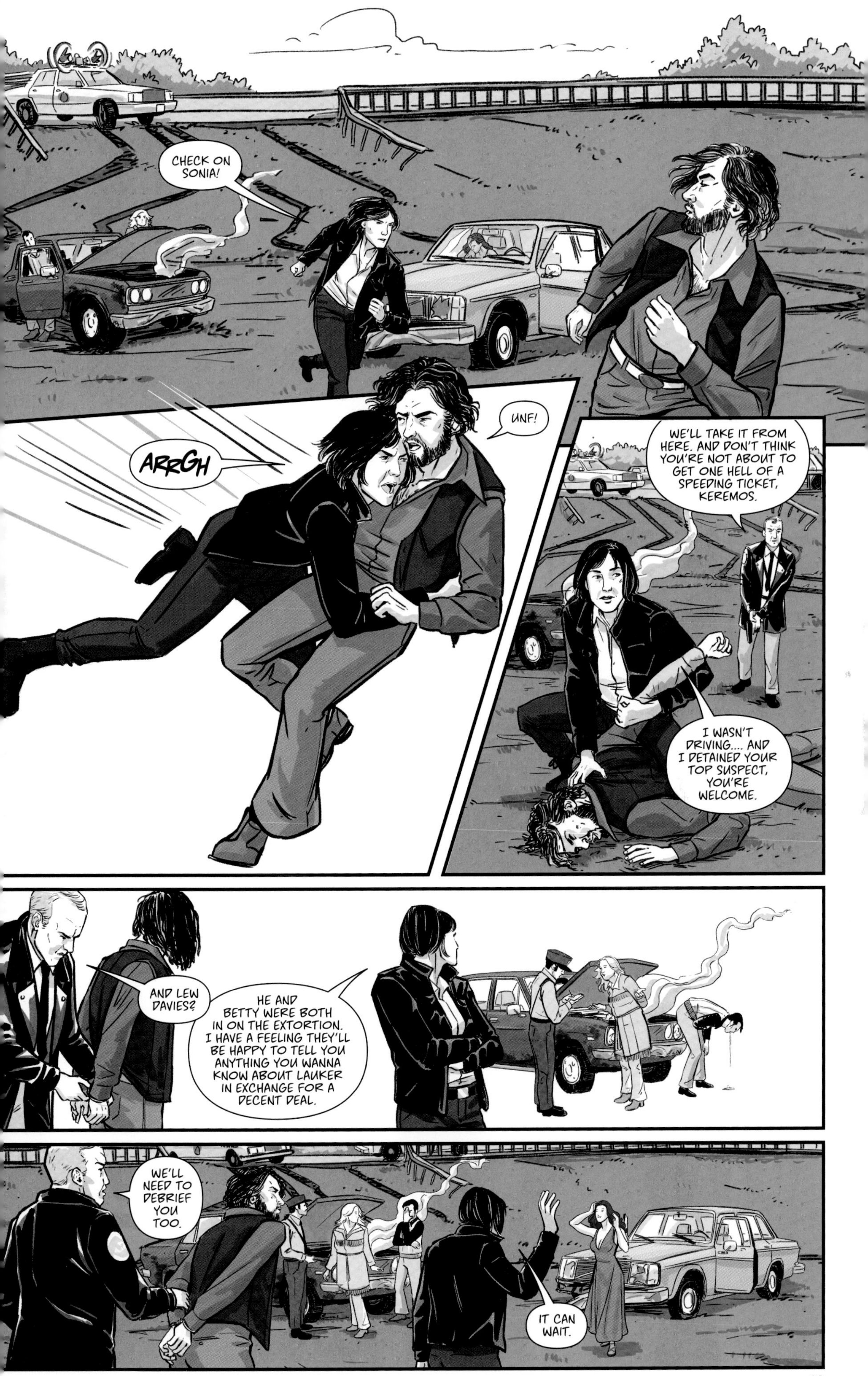
CHECK ON SONIA!
ARRGH
UNF!
WE'LL TAKE IT FROM HERE. AND DON'T THINK YOU'RE NOT ABOUT TO GET ONE HELL OF A SPEEDING TICKET, KEREMOS.
I WASN'T DRIVING.... AND I DETAINED YOUR TOP SUSPECT, YOU'RE WELCOME.
AND LEW DAVIES?
HE AND BETTY WERE BOTH IN ON THE EXTORTION. I HAVE A FEELING THEY'LL BE HAPPY TO TELL YOU ANYTHING YOU WANNA KNOW ABOUT LAUKER IN EXCHANGE FOR A DECENT DEAL.
WE'LL NEED TO DEBRIEF YOU TOO.
IT CAN WAIT.

OH HELEN, I WAS SO SCARED!

YOU DID GREAT. WE COULDN'T HAVE CAUGHT UP WITH YOU IF YOU HADN'T FOUGHT LAUKER IN THE CAR... THAT WAS DAMN BRAVE.

UH, LOOKS LIKE WE GOT $100,000 CASH IN A BAG IN HERE.

THAT SHOULD BE $200 UNLESS... CHESTER.

YOU MIGHT WANNA SEND SOME GUYS BACK TO THE HOTEL TO PICK UP THE HOUSE DICK. HE'LL BE THE GUY WITH A LOT OF CASH.

THE HOTEL DETECTIVE. HE'DA SOLD HIS OWN MOTHER FOR $100,000. THAT EXPLAINS HOW WALTER KNEW WE WERE GONE, AND THAT RONNIE HAD A BACKPACK.

BUT, HE'S A DETECTIVE!

YEAH, WELL. THE WORLD IS FULL OF DECENT PEOPLE, DOLL, BUT VERY FEW OF THEM ARE IN THE DETECTIVE BUSINESS.

AND SOME ARE MORE THAN DECENT. I WAS THINKING...YOU'VE GOT A NEW TRUCK COMING THANKS TO THE INSURANCE MONEY, AND YOUR FEE FROM ME. WHAT'S NEXT?

WELL, I HAD BEEN PLANNING A ROAD TRIP TO VANCOUVER BUT...

YOU KNOW, I'VE NEVER DONE A TRIP LIKE THAT... A TRUCK AND TENT AND ALL THE TIME IN THE WORLD SOUND LIKE A NICE CHANGE OF PACE. ANY CHANCE YOU'D LIKE SOME COMPANY?

SURE, THAT WOULD BE GREAT.

AND IT WAS...
BUT THAT'S
ANOTHER
STORY.

Afterword

by **SELENA GOULDING**

I've been working as an illustrator in one way or another for about ten years now, but around the beginning of 2018, I found myself at a low, unsatisfied with my work and uncertain if I'd continue as an artist. Luckily, that's when *Work for a Million* found me, or I found it.

When the call for artist submissions went out, I found myself excited and hopeful for the first time in ages. While I hadn't read the original novels, the premise of a period, hard-boiled lesbian detective story set in my adopted home of Toronto excited me like no other. I knew I had to be a part of it, and sent in my portfolio with bated breath. Somehow, the stars aligned and I was brought on to the team, and then came the hard part: drawing the thing.

Toronto—Canada as a whole, really—has never been as in love with documenting its changing face as American urban centres, so it wasn't always easy picturing what the city had been like before I was even born. What had changed? What had stayed the same? What did a Toronto police car look like? To be honest, I really had no idea. It was important to myself and the whole team that the graphic novel paint an authentic picture, so I set to work discovering the Toronto of the not-quite-recent past.

Luckily, despite the constant bloom of condos downtown, the old Toronto I discovered was a mostly familiar place. Things have definitely changed—updates to our transit systems, for example. For this, the Toronto Reference Library was an invaluable resource; I really don't know where this graphic novel would be without it!

Finally, I just wanted to say how wonderful it was to work with the whole creative team. The road was rocky at times, but we got there. I know we all put in our best work. It was a labour of love for all of us, and we hope you all enjoy it!

Historical Research

Artist Selena Goulding extensively researched aspects of 1970s Toronto life in order to bring to life the vivid time travel of this graphic novel. From clothing to hairstyles, interior design, and subway cars, reference from newspaper archives and magazines provided the bulk of the reference images used to create this world.

TORONTO SUBWAY

In the 1970s, Toronto was hit with a string of racial attacks on the subway system, the Toronto Transit Commission (TTC). As a result, ads were created to try to help create positive feelings while riding the train. The design of interior spaces, as well as many of Toronto's exterior and crowd scenes, were helped by the extensive visual archives provided by the Toronto Public Library, both online and in person.

ROOMING HOUSE

In the 1970s, increased attention was paid to the conditions of rooming houses—not so much regarding the comfort of the inhabitants but the fears for the safety of the neighbourhoods around the houses. While the insides may have changed, the exteriors of these buildings in Toronto's inner neighbourhoods are largely the same as they were fifty years ago and older, and were the inspiration for Uncle Karl's flophouse.

RECORDING STUDIO

Visual Researcher Pamela Grimaud provided reference images of Le Studio (Perry Sound Studio), where Rush recorded many of their songs. In a spot of luck, the studio was available "for sale" at the time and had remained largely unchanged over the last forty years, providing an excellent set of interior reference images from the for-sale ad!

SONIA'S DRESSING GOWN

Sonia's dressing gown is actually a purposeful throwback, out of tune with the more comfortable lingerie of the 1970s, chosen purposefully to reflect her particular Classic Hollywood style. It's based on classic marabou and fur dressing gowns of the 1930s and 40s, but you can still buy modern reproductions today from companies and burlesque designers.

WOMEN'S PROTEST

The creator of Helen Keremos, Eve Zaremba, has been a passionate advocate for women's and lesbian rights in Toronto. As a nod to her activist history, our heroes Helen and Alex pass by a women's march in Toronto. Inspiration for the signs was taken from various women's marches that happened across North America in the late 1970s. Project Manager Ottie Lockey provided some of the poster-board headlines from her memories of the marches.

NATE OTTOLINE

Helen's friend Nate Ottoline is a mover and shaker in the music industry in Toronto, and as such, would have a cool, impressive aura around him. We went with inspiration from different avenues, one being the Canadian Black rights activist Rosie Douglas, who was deported to Dominica in the 1970s after being arrested for taking part in a political sit-in for Black student rights. Another was the Black Panther Party band The Lumpen.

Character Sketches

by SELENA GOULDING

Helen Keremos

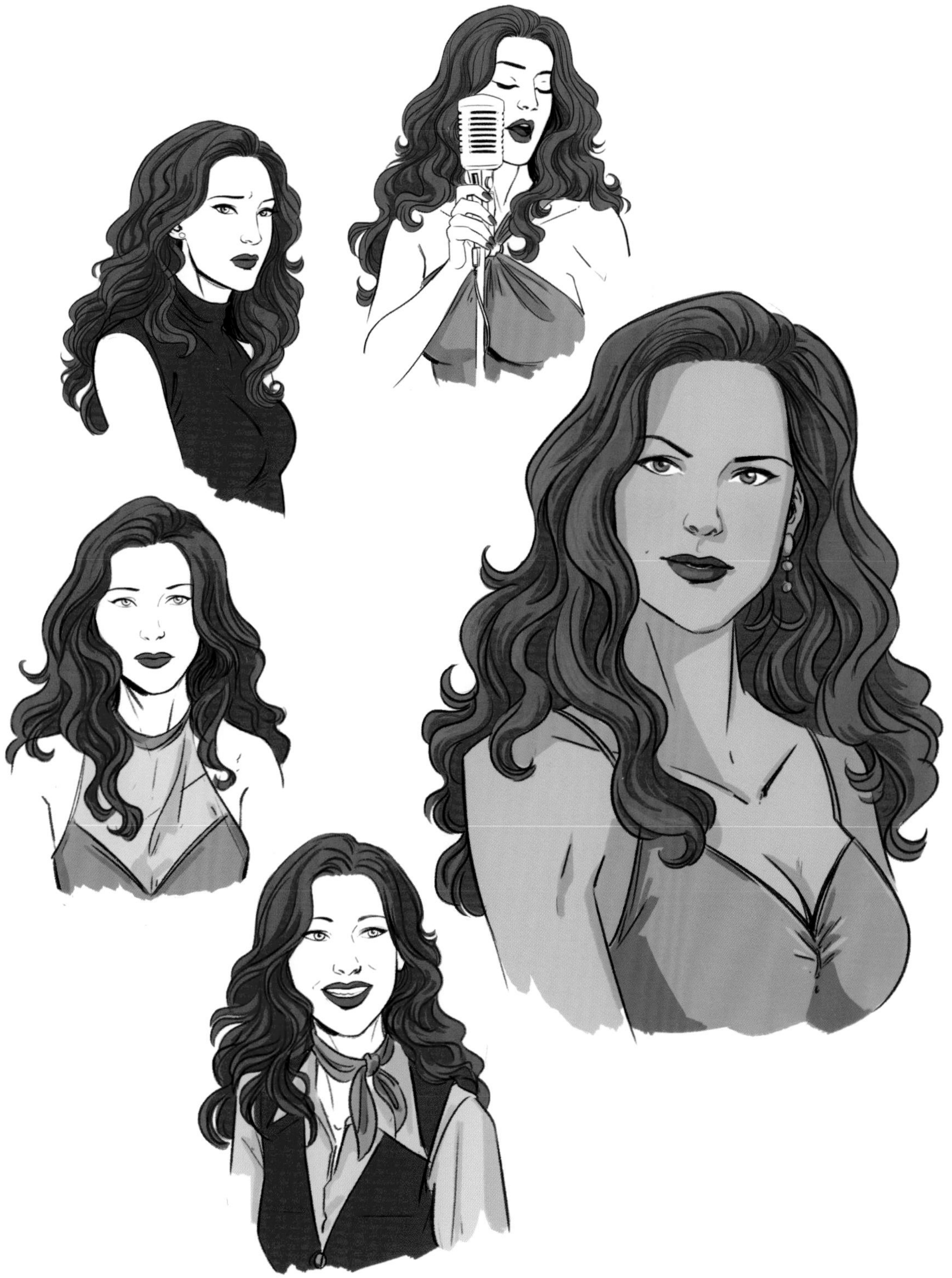

Sonia Deerfield

Helen Keremos

Sonia Deerfield

Arthur Sedgwick

Betty Grelick

Lew Davies **Alex Edwards**

Walt Lauker   **Karl Deerfield**

Ben Bono   **Nate Ottoline**   **Detective Sergeant Malory**

Helen Keremos Returns!

by OTTIE LOCKEY

When Eve and I first met over forty years ago, I was intrigued by her dyke detective who starred in a series of mysteries much like the hard-boiled pulp mysteries of past decades. Eve's heroine, Helen Keremos, was brave, bold, and unconventional. At a time when genre fiction with lesbian, gay, or queer characters usually ended badly, Helen was successful both in solving cases and in romance.

Work for a Million was first published in 1987, and feminists, lesbians, gays, and queers all caught on pretty quickly. The mystery was thoughtfully crafted, blending noir atmosphere with the modern sensibilities of the 80s, but it was discarded by mainstream critics. Fans still write to Eve to this day, thanking her for the role model she created decades ago. I always loved the character and Eve's deftly plotted mysteries, and I saw Helen as the star of a film or TV series someday.

Finally, thirty five years later, we have a reboot with a graphic novel! Eve's mystery inspired Selena Goulding and Amanda Deibert to create a graphic novel showcasing this strong lesbian hero in a new medium. I am thrilled to see Helen come to life, especially since the story has been so cleverly adapted and the characters are so beautifully rendered. The story of Helen protecting a beautiful singer, saving her from danger, and just possibly going off into the sunset together is ideally suited to the graphic novel format.

As more or less a newcomer to the world of comix and graphic novels, I found the milieu, creators, and fans to be exciting additions to my cultural life. I started buying books like Seth's *Clyde Fans*, *Berlin* by Jason Lutes, and of course, Margaret Atwood's Angel Catbird series. With Selena Goulding as my guide, I even ventured through the jam-packed Toronto Comic Arts Festival for the first time. What a mind blowing experience that was—it felt like the Toronto Reference Library held thousands and thousands of fans who were in a semi-ecstatic state. I held on to Selena and, with her help, found dozens of books I wanted to read.

I hope you have enjoyed this graphic novel adaptation of Eve's *Work for a Million* as much as I've enjoyed being part of the creative team. It's been a delight to see how much young people today relate to the characters and scenes Eve's imagined over thirty five years ago. Thanks to all the Kickstarter fans who helped make this book possible! If you are curious about the original mystery, you can find a new edition of *Work for a Million* published by Amanita and Second Story Press. And, last but not least, thanks from the creative team to the dedicated and skilled team at McClelland & Stewart, including Jared Bland, Kimberlee Hesas, and Samantha North.

Creator Bios

AMANDA DEIBERT *(WRITER)*: Amanda Deibert is a *New York Times* bestselling comic book and television writer. Her comic book writing includes the *New York Times* bestselling series *DC Super Hero Girls*, *Teen Titans Go!*, *Wonder Woman '77*, *Batman and Harley Quinn*, *Sensation Comics Featuring Wonder Woman*, *Wonder Women of History*, *Flash Facts*, *The Doomed and The Damned,* and *Love is Love* (*NYT* #1 Bestseller) for DC Comics, stories in *John Carpenter's Tales for A Halloween Night* volumes 2, 3, 4, 5 & 6 for Storm King Comics, and various other comics for Dark Horse and IDW. Her television credits include work for CBS, SyFy, OWN, PIVOT, HULU, QUIBI, and four years as the writer for former Vice President of the United States Al Gore on his international climate broadcast, *24 Hours of Reality*. She is currently writing for the animated series *He-Man and the Masters of the Universe* for Netflix. She lives in Los Angeles with her wife, illustrator Cat Staggs and their adorable daughter, Vivienne.

SELENA GOULDING *(ARTIST)*: Selena Goulding is a Canadian illustrator and comic book artist from Vancouver Island currently living in Toronto. A graduate from the Sequential Arts Program at Toronto's Max the Mutt Animation School, she is best known for her work on young adult indie comics such as *Cobble Hill*, publishing with 215 Ink. *Susanna Moodie: Roughing It in the Bush* was her first full-length graphic novel, based on a story by Carol Shields and published by Second Story Press in 2016. Her illustration work has also been showcased in the Dark Horse Comics anthology, *The Secret Loves of Geek Girls*.

EVE ZAREMBA *(CREATOR)*: Eve Zaremba is the author of six mystery novels featuring lesbian P.I. Helen Keremos. Active in the Women's Liberation Movement in the seventies and eighties, Zaremba was a founding member of the Broadside Collective which produced a monthly feminist paper in Toronto from 1979 to 1989. She has written articles and reviews in a number of other publications. In 1972, Zaremba selected and edited an early work of feminist non-fiction, *The Privilege of Sex, A Century of Canadian Women* (Anansi).

Born in Poland, Zaremba emigrated to Canada in 1952 after a stint in the United Kingdom; she graduated from the University of Toronto in 1963. Over the years, Zaremba has made a living in advertising, marketing, real estate, and publishing. While writing two of her novels, she ran a used bookstore in Toronto. Zaremba is a long-standing member of The Writers Union of Canada (TWUC). She lives in Toronto with her spouse Ottie Lockey, a filmmaker, arts consultant, and coach. Lockey commissioned the graphic novel adaptation of *Work for a Million* in 2017 and guided its development through a Kickstarter campaign and eventual publication by McClelland & Stewart.

Library and Archives Canada Cataloguing in Publication

Title: Work for a million / Eve Zaremba ; adapted by Amanda Deibert ; illustrated by Selena Goulding.
Names: Deibert, Amanda, author. | Goulding, Selena, illustrator. | Graphic novelization
of (work): Zaremba, Eve. Work for a million.
Description: Graphic novel adaptation of the novel Work for a Million by Eve Zaremba.
Identifiers: Canadiana (print) 20200336401 | Canadiana (ebook) 20200336428 | ISBN 9780771098338 (softcover) | ISBN 9780771098345 (EPUB)
Subjects: LCGFT: Graphic novels. | LCGFT: Graphic novel adaptations. | LCGFT: Lesbian comics. | LCGFT: Detective and mystery comics.
Classification: LCC PN6727.D45 W67 2021 | DDC 741.5/973—dc23

Edited by: Steenz
Additional edits by: Nyala Ali
Lettering by: Ed Dukeshire
Noir consultation by: Alex Segura
Art assists by: Jason Loo & James Green
Visual research by: Pamela Grimaud
Project managed by: Ottie Lockey

Cover design by Talia Abramson
Cover art by Selena Goulding
Printed and bound in China

McClelland & Stewart,
a division of Penguin Random House Canada Limited,
a Penguin Random House Company
www.penguinrandomhouse.ca

1   2   3   4   5   25   24   23   22   21